MURDER NEEDS IMAGINATION

Roderic Jeffries titles available from
Severn House Large Print

Murder Delayed
A Sunny Disappearance
An Air of Murder
An Intriguing Murder
Seeing is Deceiving

MURDER NEEDS IMAGINATION

Roderic Jeffries

Severn House Large Print
London & New York

This first large print edition published 2008
in Great Britain and the USA by
SEVERN HOUSE PUBLISHERS LTD.,
9-15 High Street, Sutton, Surrey, SM1 1DF.
First world regular print edition published 2007 by
Severn House Publishers, London and New York.

British Library Cataloguing in Publication Data

Jeffries, Roderic, 1926-
    Murder needs imagination. - Large print ed.
    1. Alvarez, Enrique (Fictitious character) - Fiction
    2. Police - Spain - Majorca - Fiction 3. Detective and
    mystery stories 4. Large type books
    I. Title
    823.9'14[F]

    ISBN-13: 978-0-7278-7683-6

Printed and bound in Great Britain by
MPG Books Ltd, Bodmin, Cornwall.

One

Gloria, seated on a wicker chair on the small balcony outside the sitting room of the penthouse flat, stared at the bay whose travel-poster blue water glinted in the sharp sunlight. 'Isn't that Jasper's yacht in the middle?'

Rowena did not answer.

'I wonder who he has on it today?'

'Not *on it*, who is *aboard her*.'

'People get so snobby about boat language. Trying to make everyone else feel infra dig, I suppose.'

'If there's a proper way of saying something, why not say it? Unless one thinks it's modern to sound half educated.'

'Do you know why a boat is always feminine?'

'Ask Frank and he'll tell you it's because without a man at the helm, she gets taken aback and drifts.'

'Have you noticed how Frank is becoming cruder and always sneering at women?'

'He's married to Enid, isn't he?' Rowena said as she stood. 'Another sherry?'

'Just a small one. It really is delicious. What brand?'

'Amontillado del Duque.'

'Never heard of it. I must get some, except I suppose it's expensive?'

'Isn't everything these days?' Rowena went through to the sitting room and refilled the schooners from the bottle on the silver salver on the table. She returned to the balcony, sat down.

Rowena said, 'I really envy you, living here, overlooking the bay. When I stare out of the windows in our place, all I can see are other rabbit-hutch bungalows. I told Ivor when we came here and were looking around that I wanted a house on its own with land around it. We were shown a *finca*. The house was a mess because it had been lived in by Mallorquins, but it could have been turned into something presentable. Ivor said that by the time it was done up to my taste, it would cost too great a proportion of our capital. Husbands can be so bloody selfish.'

'Which is why I got rid of Malcolm.'

'Do you ever hear from him?'

'Not long ago, he wrote to say he'd run into money problems and asked if I would accept a smaller income until he'd sorted everything out? Of course I instructed my solicitor to tell him to pay up and shut up.'

As Rowena replaced her glass on the table, she said, 'D'you think he's short of cash because he's found someone else?'

'Naturally. He needs a woman to tell him what a clever, handsome bastard he is.'

'Rather like Jasper.'

'Nothing like. Jasper's too damned arrogantly self-satisfied to need to be told anything.'

'Eric was complaining the other day that he'd been incredibly rude to him.'

'Eric shouldn't try to socially crawl quite as hard as he does.'

'He is a bit that way. But when one talks to

him, he can be quite interesting.'

'If one wants reviews of the past week's telly programmes.'

Gloria stared out at the bay once more. 'I think that big yacht with the striped sails is Jasper's.'

'Why so interested?'

'Just curious.'

'I'd have thought you'd know whether or not it's his.'

'Why d'you say that?' Gloria asked in a sharper voice.

'You've often been on it.'

'Who told you that lie?'

'Someone. I've forgotten who.'

'When you remember, tell your curtain-twitcher she needs her eye sight tested and her tongue chained.'

'You seem upset.'

'What d'you expect when you're told you've been out with a man who only keeps his trousers on in public? You can also tell her that the twice I *have* been on the yacht, I made certain, unlike Joan, that I wasn't on my own.'

'You wouldn't have been with him

aboard.'

'That's a bitchy thing to say.'

'Only being pedantic... And which Joan are you referring to?'

'Joan Langley. You've heard the rumours about her?'

'I never listen to them unless they blacken someone I like.'

'She constantly goes sailing with Jasper and most times there are only the two of them aboard.'

'That's one rumour you can bury. Jasper's taste is for women who are sharp and sexy, not suburban housewives.'

'I know that, but I suppose you've heard that Gavin's lost most of his money?'

'Yes.'

'Terrible luck.'

'Lend money to a friend and you deserve to lose it.'

'He and Joan are now having to watch every cent. Betty was asked to dinner recently and went expecting a slap-up meal because Joan's a good cook, but she says the meal wasn't any better than a *menu del dia* at a local restaurant because Joan couldn't afford to buy proper ingredients... I wonder if she keeps sailing with Jasper in the hopes of netting some of his money? What defeats me is what keeps him interested in her. Can she offer something special?'

'Suburban sauce with the main dish.'

Two

Alvarez was enjoying his breakfast – an *ensaimada* and hot chocolate – when the phone rang.

'Something's happened to them,' Dolores said shrilly. She hurried into the *entrada* to answer the call.

Alvarez dunked a piece of *ensaimada* into the hot chocolate. Twenty minutes earlier, Juan and Isabel had left to go by school bus to an exhibition of ancient toys in Palma. Until they returned safely, Dolores would be haunted by fears of the disasters which might befall them all the time they were beyond the safety of Llueso.

She returned. 'It's for you.' Her voice was calm once more.

'Are you sure?'

11

'You are not Inspector Alvarez of the Cuerpo?'

'Who's shouting for me?'

'One of the *cabos*. Jorge.'

'What's got him ringing this early in the morning?'

'Perhaps he does not find it as early as you do.'

'Did he say what's up?'

'No.'

'You didn't ask?'

'I mind my own business.'

As Dolores had done earlier, he considered all the bad news he might be about to hear. He reluctantly left the kitchen and went through to the *entrada*, picked up the receiver. 'Yes?'

'How are things, Enrique?'

'Getting worse by the minute. What's the trouble?'

'No time for a chat? Someone from the policia has phoned through to say a foreigner, name of...' He had difficulty in pronouncing the names Jasper Vickers, and so spelled them out. 'He's fallen three metres on to his head.'

'Dead?'

'You think he stood up and said he had a bit of a bruise?'

'Where did it happen?'

'In his home.'

'Ring the policia back and remind them that fatal accidents are their problem if there's nothing unusual.'

'The doctor who was called to examine the stiff must reckon there's something that is unusual. He said you had to be called.'

'Which doctor is it?'

'Llabres.'

'He won't diagnose a cold without talking about double pneumonia. Where's the address?'

'Ca Na Pantella. It's up the Vall del Gnomos, so don't forget a bunch of carrots.' Jorge laughed.

Some people were easily amused. The valley was so named because folklore held that gnomes had once lived in it and if a man gave them a bunch of carrots, they would instruct him on how to obtain the favours of a woman. Why carrots – why any man from Llueso should need such instruction – was not recorded.

'By the way, the doc says you're to get along there half an hour ago because he's in a hurry.'

Alvarez replaced the receiver and returned to the kitchen to finish his breakfast.

The valley was one of many that cut into the length of the Serra de Tramuntana. It was sometimes described as being in the shape of a *pimiento*. The rock faces were steep and at their highest point rose to nine hundred and thirty metres. On the eastern slopes pines grew; on the western slopes, there was not one. The gnomes were blamed.

The soil was rocky and of poor quality. A mule cart took an hour to reach the nearest village, and so even after it was generally accepted that one would not be at risk from gnomes furious at being disturbed, few Mallorquins had chosen to live there. The last small rock-built *finca* had been abandoned at the beginning of the Civil War.

Following the advent of foreign visitors, in the mid-sixties a retired German industrialist and his wife, both far more interested in exploring than lying on a beach, had toured the remoter parts of the island in a clapped-out Seat 1500 – the only medium-sized car then available on hire. On the fourth day, they had driven into Vall del Gnomos along a rutted dirt track which had the car lurching and its suspension screeching. Halfway to the virtually sheer rock face at the end, they had stopped and, in the shadow of a ruined house, picnicked. The solitude, the silence except for bird songs, and the swirl of sunlight on rock captivated them and they had decided to buy as much land as possible and have a house built. The men who had worked on the house had never understood how anyone could be so stupid as to spend a fortune in order to live in the middle of nowhere.

As the number of visiting foreigners increased, it was inevitable that there would be a few for whom the remoteness and solitude was a bonus, not a liability. Three more houses were built in the valley and the newest and largest of these was Ca Na Pantella.

Alvarez parked his Ibiza behind the tricoloured policia Ford and a Renault Mégane. He climbed out and studied the valley. Sharp crests which imagination could turn into recognizable forms, stark grandeur of rock, even the poor earth spattered with large and small rocks, possessed an attraction for those who preferred nature's works to humans.

He crossed to the elaborate wrought-iron gateway and went into the garden. Good earth had been imported – necessarily, regardless of cost – and there were flower beds, a lawn, jacaranda and mimosa trees, nurtured by the water from a well, successfully drilled where no stranger to the island would expect there to be a subterranean source of water.

The front door was made of dark, rich wood, patterned in traditional squares. He opened it and stepped into a spacious hall with a ceiling five metres high and, at the far end, an open gallery. Below the gallery lay a body with a sheet over it. He could never look at death, covered or not, without icily remembering his own mortality.

Fullano, in policia uniform, stepped out of

the room to the right. 'Good to see you, Enrique.'

Fullano was an old acquaintance and they exchanged domestic news at length before Alvarez pointed at the body. 'What's the story?'

'Ana, the maid, started work by going up the back stairs to check the sitting room, which is upstairs. There were two empty bottles of gin, suggesting a good booze-up, and apparently a bit of the carpet was damp so she did what she could with that. She took the bottles down the back stairs, realized it was time to ask the *señor* what he wanted for breakfast – always had it in bed, like some great pasha, when on his own...'

'Which pashas seldom were.'

'Sounds like the *señor* wasn't that often, either. Anyway, she went back upstairs, knocked on the bedroom door, no answer. Knocked twice more and then – nervously, ready to run, I'd say – she looked inside; no *señor* in bedroom, bathroom, or study. She put the tray down on the dressing table, returned down the front stairs into the hall, saw the body and screamed.

'Elena, the cook, calmed her down – from the look of Elena, she could calm a rampaging bull – called Diaz, the gardener, and he phoned us. We got in touch with the duty doctor. He examined the body, said you had to be called in.'

'Did he say why?'

'No.'

'Where is he now?'

'In what they call the morning room – bit of an odd name, that. Aren't you allowed in it in the afternoon? And talking about pashas, he thinks he's one. Told Ana he wanted coffee as if he paid her wages. I've heard his wife is even more arrogant than him, but that's difficult to believe.'

'I suppose I'd better find out what he's got to say.'

'It won't be a polite "good morning". Came out ten minutes ago and demanded to know if you were coming here on a bicycle.'

'Where is the morning room?'

'Second door on the left.' Fullano pointed.

Alvarez crossed the hall, passing further

18

from the covered body than was necessary, opened the door and stepped into a large, oblong room, furnished extensively without great taste. He would have called it a sitting room. The large picture window provided a view to the end of the valley and the steep, at times precipitous, rock faces that formed it.

Llabres was small and precisely shaped. His sharply featured face expressed more arrogance than a desire to serve humanity; his mousy moustache denoted the lack of a sense of humour. 'Are you from the Cuerpo?' he asked, the pitch of his voice surprisingly deep.

'Inspector Alvarez, Doctor.'

He picked up a cup from the tray on an occasional table, drank, replaced it. 'I have been waiting a very long time. Were you not told to get here immediately?'

'Yes, but I'm afraid I sometimes face the same problem as you must in your work.'

'Most unlikely.'

'You don't have to decide priorities? You surely wouldn't leave a dying man to deal with a sore throat?'

19

'I find that remark insulting and ridiculous.'

Alvarez was gratified this was so. He had expected to be asked to sit, but had not been; so he sat on one of four comfortable chairs. 'I understand you believe Señor Vickers's death was not an accident?'

'Then you believe incorrectly.'

'But if you accept it was an accident, why ask me to come here?'

'It is not for me to decide whether or not it was an accident, just as it is not your job to question my demand for you to be here. Your presence is required so that you can be shown certain important features.'

'In what way important?'

'Again you will decide, not I.' Llabres brought a handkerchief from a trouser pocket, carefully brushed his lips. He stood, replaced the handkerchief. 'Follow me.'

A bantam cockerel, Alvarez thought, as he followed into the hall; crowing loudly enough to make him believe he was twice the man he was.

Llabres came to a halt a metre from the body. 'Uncover him.'

Alvarez pulled back the sheet. His feeling of nausea was immediate, followed by his indignation that death could be so primitive.

'The injuries suffered are consistent with his having fallen from the gallery above.' Llabres spoke as if addressing students. 'There is the point of contact.' He pointed.

Several centimetres to the right of the head was an irregular patch of dried blood, already darkened, and other substances which Alvarez did not wish to identify. One tile had been cracked.

'Confirmation that the fall resulted in his death will be provided by the post-mortem.'

'Can you give a time of death?'

'Between midnight and two hundred hours this morning is my best estimate. These times are to be regarded as indicative, not definitive. You understand that?' He seemed worried that Alvarez might be unable to do so. 'Examine the neck.'

Alvarez unwillingly leaned over to do so.

'Good God, man, you're not going to see anything from up there. Crouch down. Now tell me what you can observe.'

After uncomfortably hunkering down, he saw dead skin over dead flesh and bones.

'There are two shallow, horizontal cuts on the neck below the chin. Can you say when these were made?'

'Not long before death. How long, it is impossible to judge.'

'What caused them?'

'I am not a soothsayer.'

'A knife?'

'If it had a finely edged blade and was pressed only lightly against the skin.'

'Could the cuts have been caused when shaving?'

'Is it normal for a man to shave his neck horizontally rather than vertically?'

'Perhaps when he was shaving, something caught his attention, he held the razor still, but turned his head and neck to try to determine what that something was.'

'The two cuts are less than a centimetre apart and almost parallel. You can imagine he twice had his attention caught, twice turned his head without lifting the razor off his neck, despite having cut himself the first time?'

'It was just a quick thought.'

'Ebarno reminds one that to think quickly is often to think without thought.'

And to sneer was the pleasure of an empty mind. 'Do you judge the cuts were made by a knife, or something similar?'

'I say no more than I have already done. You will now observe the mouth.'

The lips were slightly parted. Perhaps Vickers had been trying to shout his anger at dying.

'What do you notice?'

'The lips seem to be slightly swollen on the right-hand side. That is, to the right when facing them.'

'Have you looked inside the mouth?'

'No.'

'You do not believe in examining every detail?'

He did not believe in examining a dead man's mouth.

'A tooth – in ignorant parlance, the lower right-hand eye tooth – has been loosened.'

'He suffered a blow to his mouth?'

'I would expect a blow from a fist or some other object to cause a wider area of injury.'

'Then what do you imagine happened?'

'I do not imagine; I restrict myself to facts.'

Alvarez stood, finding that more difficult than it should have been. Dolores frequently told him he was getting old – too old to run after young women, was what she really meant. She harboured unjustified suspicions...

'You will examine the wrists.'

Why couldn't the wretched man have said that before he stood? He once more, painfully, knelt.

'What do you see?'

'Nothing. Nothing unusual, that is.'

'You fail to notice the hairs on the wrists?'

After a careful visual search he saw that on each wrist, the hairs had been stripped away for roughly five centimetres and that the upper line was horizontally straight. 'Were they tied together with masking tape, or something else that tore out the hairs when stripped free?'

'That is a possibility.'

'Can you suggest another?'

'No.'

'You are saying that they were bound?'

'I am saying no more than that your suggestion is one possibility. There will be others, but I am not called upon to name them.'

Were his patients often told what they *might* be suffering from?

'I am finished,' Llabres said. 'I will return and try to catch up on some of the time you have caused me to lose.' He picked up his medical bag, walked with strutting stride to the outside door, and left.

If he judged solely on what Llabres had said, Alvarez decided, this was a case of accident, murder, or perhaps even alien intervention. He sought Fullano and found him in the kitchen. 'Where's the photographer?'

'Riding here on his bicycle.' Fullano laughed.

'Ring up and find out what's happening.'

'Why the rush? He said he'd be as quick as he could, so there's no point in phoning. And since I can't be of any more use, I'm on my way.'

'But I have to—'

'And so do I. Find Elena and ask her to

make you some coffee and give you a slice of her chocolate sponge. It's the best you'll ever taste and it'll keep your mind off your problems.'

Three

Fullano had not exaggerated. As Alvarez regretfully ate the last piece of the second slice of cake, he knew that not even Dolores could cook such a tongue-pleasing, stomach-warming chocolate sponge.

'Have some more,' Elena said.

He cut a large slice.

'And you'd like another coffee?'

She refilled his cup, passed it and the bottle of Carlos I across the table.

She might look formidable – heavily built and with features designed for hectoring rather than murmuring sweet endearments – and her manner and speech might often be brusque to the point of rudeness, but she knew what pleased a man.

'You can tell me about the *señor*,' he said

before he resumed eating.

She sat opposite him and rested her elbows on the table. Her very generous breasts, only loosely contained, did the same.

'You must be shocked by his death?'

'Naturally.'

She had spoken unemotionally. She was from a background of generations who accepted death had to follow life.

'Was he married?'

'Not as far as any of us know.'

'Then there's no family?'

'Who can say if there are a few of his bastards here and there.' She spoke with typical Mallorquin bluntness.

'He liked the women?'

'And they liked his money.'

Contrary to tradition, money did buy happiness. 'What about men?'

'What about them?'

'Did he like them along with the women? Some men have divided pleasures.'

'It wasn't his pleasures he divided all the time.'

'What about a little S and M?'

'Much too scared of pain,' she answered

scornfully. 'He cracked a rib on that boat of his and for the next month you'd have thought he'd broken every bone in his body.'

He hesitated, then cut himself another, smaller, piece of sponge. This provoked the memory of his doctor telling him that if he didn't eat and drink less, and give up smoking, he wouldn't make old bones. All doctors should be christened Jeremiah. 'What was the *señor* like as an employer?'

'If things were as he wanted them, he could be pleasant; if things weren't, he'd shout his head off. And he was so nervous, there was usually something to complain about. Got a lot worse recently.'

'Why?'

'How would I know? Started complaining about everything. The house was dusty when it wasn't; he told Diaz the flowers weren't being watered properly and accused Ana of stealing a pen from his desk and had her in tears, the poor girl; he even complained about my cooking!'

'Then his mind had become affected. What d'you think caused this change?'

'Haven't I just said? I don't know.' She

stood. 'I must start...' Her expression became uneasy. She slowly sat once more. 'There was me thinking I had to start cooking for him. Won't be wanting anything today or any other day. What's more, me, Ana and Diaz had better start looking for another job.'

'Wait until the place is sold, offer the new owner some chocolate sponge and he'll beg you to stay on and will double your wages.'

She smiled briefly.

'Did the *señor* entertain a lot?'

'All the time. Didn't matter what we thought.'

'You're talking of women?'

'Of course I am.'

'What about friends and acquaintances?'

'Sometimes, but not all that often. If you ask me, he didn't get on well with ordinary people.'

'Of those who did come here, were the majority foreigners or Mallorquins?'

'Didn't have anything to do with us Mallorquins.'

'Was there a visitor last night?'

'Not as far as I know.'

'You can't be certain?'

She removed elbows and breasts from the table, leaned back in the chair. 'Are you thinking maybe it wasn't an accident?' The thought did not appear to upset her.

'I have to check every possibility.'

'There'll be more than one husband who will smile to know he's dead.'

'Name some names.'

'You think his women were introduced to me?'

'When did you last see the *señor*?'

'After supper I cleared up, because Ana was away with that man of hers. I've told her often enough that from the look of him, she needs to be careful. She just laughs. Says she learned enough when she was at school. Things weren't like that when we were young and mothers guarded their daughters until the day they married.'

And modern male youth did not realize how lucky they were to enjoy modern freedom. 'What was the time when you cleared up?'

She thought for a while. 'Ten, like as not.'

'And then you did what?'

31

'Went back to the staff house which is where Ana and me live. Diaz is married so he goes home.'

'That's the small house halfway along the drive?'

'Yes.'

'Can you hear cars drive past and come up here, to the house?'

'Mostly.'

'Did you hear one last night?'

'Only Ana returning.'

'When was that?'

'Can't rightly say.'

'Have a guess.'

'Wasn't long after I went to bed and I remember thinking, for once she's back at a respectable time. Usually doesn't get back until there's no need to wonder what she's been up to.'

'When did you go to bed?'

'Eleven, same as I always do.'

'So she was back before half past eleven?'

'I suppose.'

'Did you hear her enter the staff house?'

'No. The minx moves so quietly because she doesn't want me to know when she returns.'

'That seems to be everything, so thanks for helping. I'd better have a word with Ana now.'

'You can't.'

'Why's that?'

'She's in a state after seeing him in such a mess, that's why.'

He could sympathize. 'I'll have a word with her another time. But before I leave, I'll have a look around.'

'Around where?'

'This house.'

Despite the need to return home in good time – Dolores had started cooking before he left and the smells had suggested something good, possibly *Romesco de Peix*, compared with which, bouillabaisse became a very ordinary fish stew – he made a careful search of the house.

There was a good security system and no sign of forced entry. The master suite consisted of a large bedroom, dressing-room and bathroom. In one of the cupboards of the bathroom was an electric razor, but nowhere was there a safety or cut-throat

razor or even shaving cream. In the bedroom, traditionally concealed behind a
painting – *Nature's Bounty* by Manuel
Ibanéz (did Ibanéz suffer from some
disorder of his sight which caused him to
see blue trees, red grass, and orange grapes?)
– was a combination safe.

The other five bedrooms were empty of
anything of interest. The sitting room had
obviously – and regrettably – been cleaned
and there were no empty bottles of gin.

Returning along the corridor to the main
staircase, he could look through a window
out to the valley. Had this house known
visitors with sufficient humility to be hum-
bled by that view?

He returned to the gallery. He imagined
Vickers, arms secured, being forced over the
banisters. Had there been time, had his
mind been sufficiently coherent, for him to
wonder what he would experience after his
head smashed on to the floor and he died?

Four

Seated in his chair in the office, Alvarez stared at the telephone to the right of the unsorted papers and unopened mail on his desk, at his watch, and then at a gecko. As it ran up the side of the window, he recalled the day, when he was young, that he had tried to catch a gecko and his mother had been frightened and warned him that if it touched his flesh it would never let go. In those days myths, however absurd, had been believed because many could not read and there had been no television to destroy them as it created others of its own making. The gnomes of Vall del Gnomos; the holy well of San Marcos, which had miraculously sprung out of rock on Midsummer's Day and the waters of which had performed many miracles; the ghosts which haunted the talyots on the Day of the Dead...

He had to accept he could prevaricate no longer, so he lifted the receiver and dialled.

'Yes?' said Salas's secretary, in her plum-filled voice, her manner even curter than usual.

'Inspector Alvarez. I should like to speak to the superior chief.'

The wait was short. 'So you are still alive!' Salas said.

'As far as I know, Señor,' he replied lightly.

'I often have my doubts.'

'I can assure you that if I am pricked, I bleed; if I am tickled, I laugh...'

'What nonsense are you talking? Do you realize that today is the tenth of June?'

He looked across at the calendar, stuck to the wall with tape, and was surprised that the month was so far advanced. Above the list of days was a photograph of workers harvesting figs to dry in the sun. The compiler of the calendar was no farmer. Figs were not picked for drying before July. And these days, very few could be bothered to undertake such laborious work. In the past, of course, when every peseta had to be pursued, the whole family would be engaged in placing the ripened fruit on wooden trays which were put under cover each night, sorting out the bad figs, turning the good ones, briefly baking them or pouring boiling water over them to kill pests; drying them again...

'Where the devil have you got to?'

'Nowhere, Señor.'

'A suitable description for the usual result of your work. Does the date mean nothing to you?'

He tried to think why it should.

'You have read and acted upon my latest order?'

'Of course, Señor.'

'Then will you explain why I have received the required form from every inspector but you?'

Not knowing what Salas was talking about, he searched amongst the litter on his desk to find the envelope in which the order would have arrived. He finally identified it by the logo of the Cuerpo, and ripped open the envelope.

'You are finding difficulty in composing an explanation I might be gullible enough to accept?'

He pulled out a single sheet of paper. From receipt of the order, each inspector was to detail all cases handled in the previous month and list the measures taken. The report was to be on the superior chief's desk by the Tuesday of the second week of the following month.

'Am I to have an answer, however absurd?'

'I sent my report by post, Señor. It should have reached you in good time.'

'You made a copy of it, as required by standing orders concerning all communications to Palma?'

'Yes, of course.'

'Then you will fax that to me. Immediately.' The line went dead.

Alvarez reached down to the bottom right-hand drawer of the desk and brought out a bottle of Soberano and a glass. There were times when alcohol was less of a pleasure than a necessity. As he poured himself a drink, the phone rang. He put the bottle down on the desk, lifted the receiver.

'The superior chief will speak to you.'

'Alvarez, you—' Salas began.

'Señor, there is a slight problem with the machine.'

'You phoned me earlier, but failed to explain why.'

'It was to tell you what had happened, Señor, in the Vickers case.'

'Then why didn't you?'

'Because before I could do so, you expressed your concern about the failure of my report to reach you in the post. I explained this had to be because the post was yet again at fault. You said—'

'I am well aware of what I said, unlike you who are often unaware of what you have, or have not, said.'

'Señor, if I don't say something, that is because I have nothing to say. As Pedro Roig wrote, "The world would be a quieter place if those who had nothing of consequence to say, said nothing." Of course, if one is literal, one can't say nothing because to do so is to say something. It's the same if one says one cannot say anything. Words can become difficult...'

'In your mouth, they become incomprehensible. Refrain from any further comments of an illiterate nature and tell me in the simplest terms why you phoned me earlier.'

'Early this morning, I was informed that Señor Vickers, an Englishman, had fallen over a balustrade and been fatally injured...'

'You are unaware that accidents are no concern of ours unless an investigation is required in order to advise on what action should be carried out so as to prevent the possibility of any repetition?'

'That is what I told the policia, but he said the doctor who had been called was insisting I appear. Naturally, I assumed there were reasons to suspect it was not a straightforward accident so I drove immediately to Ca Na Pantella.

'Initially, it appeared Doctor Llabres need not have asked me to go there. Señor Vickers had been drunk, had stumbled or tripped over the low balustrades and had fallen head first on to the tiled floor—'

'A post-mortem has already been carried out?'

'I have had no word that it has.'

'Then in the circumstances, where is the justification for saying he was drunk?'

'Two empty bottles of gin were found in the upstairs sitting room. Even for an English gentleman, that is surely enough to ensure drunkenness?'

'Empty bottles do not mean their contents were drunk by one man.'

'The staff confirm he was on his own all day. And had the bottles been there in the early evening, when the maid checked the room, she would have removed them.'

'One bottle might well have been virtually empty to begin with.'

'The torn customs labels strongly suggest both were unopened when they were put on the table.' Alvarez waited, but Salas made no further comment. 'The doctor drew my attention to certain features on the body. The lips were bruised and an eye tooth had been loosened, though not forced out of the gum. I asked him if he thought the *señor* had received a blow to the mouth; he replied that in those circumstances, he would expect there to have been a greater degree of bruising.'

'Then what does he think happened?'

'He would not give a definite opinion.'

'Typical!'

'There were two fine cuts on the dead man's neck, under his chin. I suggested they had been made by a knife. The doctor said possibly, if made with a sharp-edged one held lightly against the skin. They were a little like cuts made when shaving badly, but since they ran horizontally and not vertically, I realized this was not very feasible. Confirmation that they were not occasioned by shaving came when I examined his bathroom. He used an electric razor and there was no safety or cut-throat razor there.

'The doctor asked me to examine the wrists. I noticed that a circle of hairs were missing and when they resumed, they did so in a straight line, some a few centimetres higher. I suggested this was consistent with the wrists having been bound together with something like masking tape.'

'His answer?'

'It was possible.'

'He would not be more certain than that?'

'No, Señor.'

'Were there any other signs of bondage?'

'No... I have spoken to the cook. She could confirm that all Monday, the *señor* had been on his own until she returned to the staff cottage that night. Her further evidence was that he very frequently entertained ladies, some of whom were married.'

'That is all she could tell you?'

'Yes.'

'Because you have so poor an appreciation of logic and the value of evidence, I don't doubt you are about to claim he was murdered.'

'I don't think one can say that yet.'

'You surprise me. You have questioned all the other staff?'

'Not yet.'

'Why not?'

Because if he had returned to Ca Na Pantella, he would have been even later back to lunch than he was going to be. 'Ana, the maid, was too shocked at finding the dead man to be questioned.'

'That was the doctor's opinion?'

43

'No. But the cook said she was in a dreadful state of nerves.'

'The cook is a psychological diagnostician?'

'I thought it kinder not to question Ana until she was at least partially recovered.'

'And if the cook reports her to be too shocked tomorrow, the next day, the next week, you will accept her expert advice and refrain from questioning her?'

'I'm sure she'll get over it quite soon.'

'You will question her this afternoon. And you will report to me when you have done so.'

'Yes, Señor. There is another point I should make.'

'Which is?'

Alvarez momentarily hesitated, knowing how his words would be received. 'There is the possibility it may not be a case of murder.'

'According to what you have told me, a man is threatened with a knife, tied up, thrown downstairs to his death, but that is not murder?'

'He may have been drunkenly indulging in

44

a certain form of behaviour and things got out of hand. It is not unknown.'

'What is unknown to me is what you are talking about.'

'Bondage, fear of having one's neck sliced ... Does that not suggest a certain type of pleasure?'

'It suggests that a man who can equate such things with pleasure is in urgent need of help.'

'They are possible signs of S and M.'

'Is that supposed to mean something to me?'

'He may just have been indulging in S and M.'

'I am rapidly coming to the conclusion that you have been indulging in either drink or drugs.'

'Sado-masochism, Señor.'

There was a long silence. 'I do wonder,' Salas finally said, with some perplexity, 'whether you could investigate the theft of a bar of chocolate without introducing in your report matters of a sexual nature?'

'There has to be that possibility at this stage of the case.'

'An inescapable possibility only to a diseased mind. Unless you very regrettably uncover evidence of such unmentionable behaviour, you will not raise the matter again. Is that quite clear?' Salas rang off.

'You're late back,' Jaime said.

Alvarez sat at the dining-room table, reached across for the bottle of Fundador and a glass, poured himself a drink, added two cubes of ice. 'It's been a very stressful morning.'

Dolores stepped through the bead curtain across the kitchen doorway. 'You have had a stressful morning?'

Alvarez gloomily nodded.

'Then think how fortunate you are to be able now to relax. How every woman would like to be able to do the same! Not, of course, that the stress we women suffer can be compared to that which you men do. Our only problems are to wake up the children and make certain they wash, prepare breafast, get the children to school, clean the house, tidy the rooms in which the men seldom put anything away and when they

46

do it is in the wrong place, shop regardless of how many kilometres of walking that it takes to buy only from those shops which sell the food men prefer, cook in a kitchen which is hotter than the fires of hell because the fan still has not be repaired by a stressed husband and so each minute becomes two... And all this without a moment in which to be able to relax.

'Then, of course, when meals are finished, the table has to be cleared. And while the men enjoy a drink, or two, coffee must be made for them and then there is the washing-up of knives, forks, spoons, plates, dishes, glasses...' Her voice sharpened. 'Do either of you know what is the greatest cause of stress?"

Women, Alvarez thought.

'Alcohol.'

Jaime had never been able to judge correctly when silence was essential as well as golden. 'A drink relaxes a man.'

'Indeed. It relaxes him until he can no longer control his tongue, cannot discern, or care, whether he is eating badly cooked *garbanzos* or *costelletes de por amb salsa de magranes.*' She returned into the kitchen, autocratic head held high.

Alvarez awoke, stared up at the ceiling of his bedroom and at the bars of light and dark formed by the reflected sunlight coming through the shutters. Provided he did not look at his watch, he would not know if it was time to get up...

'Enrique,' Dolores called from downstairs, 'are you returning to work?'

'Yes.'

'Now, or tomorrow morning?'

'I'm getting dressed.'

He went downstairs and through to the kitchen, sat at the table. Dolores was chopping onions and carrots. He waited, but when she did not stop work to serve him, he said, 'Is there any coffee?'

'In the machine.'

He stood, crossed to the work surface on which sat the coffee maker, realized he needed a mug, fetched one from the cupboard near the twin sinks, filled the mug with coffee. 'Where's the sugar?'

'Where it should be.'

It should be on the table for him to help himself. He collected the plastic container from the side of the cooker, added two spoonfuls of sugar to the coffee. 'Is there any milk?'

'In the refrigerator because I have been feeling too stressed to get it out. And there is some coca, but I've forgotten where.' She put down the knife, hurried out of the kitchen.

He searched for, and found, the coca. He brought the bottle of milk out of the refrigerator, sat once more.

Dolores returned. 'Soon,' she said, as she crossed to the sinks, 'it will be so late, there will be little point in you returning to work since it will then be time to return home.'

The quality of supper might well depend on her suffering a less caustic mood. 'The coca is as light as a fairy's wings, so obviously you made it.'

'And do you know why?'

'Because you're a peerless cook—'

'Because I suffer from the stupid assumption that it is my duty, no matter at what cost to myself, to provide a home which pleases my men. Of course, they never consider the effort involved sufficiently to consider thanking me for my uncomplaining slavery.' She brought a duster out of a cupboard. 'Before you leave, put the milk back in the refrigerator, the coffee machine, the mug, plate and knife on the draining-board.'

She left. He cut himself another slice of coca. The claim that women were the equal of men had first been made years before. Since then, women, with their customary guile, had transformed the cult of equality into a right of domination.

Five

Ana stepped into the small, lightly furnished staff sitting room to the right of the kitchen. She looked nervously at Alvarez, then away. 'Elena says you want to talk to me?'

'Just a quick chat, so have a seat.' Alvarez watched her sit forward on the second, well-worn, armchair, as if about to get up and run. She would have been attractive, though not beautiful, had she not suffered from so square a chin, a physical trait frequently seen in Llueso. 'I'd like you to tell me what happened to you on Tuesday morning from the time you got up. And you must understand this is so I can gain a broad picture of events, not because there's the slightest reason to believe you know anything about the unfortunate *señor*'s death.'

She became less nervous, thanks to Alvarez's friendly manner.

'Elena says you both sleep in the staff house. When you're dressed, you walk up to here. Tell me everything from that moment.'

She had been the first to arrive, so she had unlocked the back door and deactivated the alarms...

'You're quite sure it was locked?'

'Like always at night.'

'Where is the key kept?'

'I have one, like Elena does.'

'And Diaz?'

'Doesn't get here until after breakfast so he doesn't need one.'

'Did you check the front door after you entered the house?'

'No.'

'So you can't say whether it was locked or unlocked?'

'It wasn't my job to do that.' Her nervousness increased.

'I quite understand... What happened after you entered the house?'

'Elena arrived and she'd made some pastries for us to have with the hot chocolate.'

'She's a wonderful cook.'

'Her croissants aren't so good.'

It seemed the relationship between the two women was not the sweetest, he noted. 'And after your breakfast?'

She had gone up the back stairs and into the upstairs sitting room to dust and tidy.

'You told Fullano – the policia – you found two empty bottles and two torn-off customs tabs from them on the table. The *señor* was a heavy drinker?'

'I wouldn't say that. I mean, I never saw him squiffy, not even after one of his parties when the guests sometimes had to be help-ed to their cars.'

'And gin was his favourite spirit?'

'Shouldn't think so.'

'Why d'you say that?' he asked sharply. Then, noticing that his tone had alarmed her, said, 'Sorry if I sounded fierce, but I'm very interested to know why you think it wasn't.'

'When there was a party, I had to hand the drinks around. He always had whisky or champagne. I gave him gin once by mistake and he was furious.'

He crossed to the large, yet shapely, heavily inlaid cocktail cabinet, opened the two doors. On the top shelf were glasses, on the bottom shelf were many bottles, amongst which were two containing Glenmorangie malt whisky. Had Vickers wished to drink whisky on the night he died, there was plenty available. 'When you came in here to make certain everything was in order, you saw the two empty bottles; was there also a dirty glass?'

She shook her head.

'Did anything strike you as unusual?'

She shook her head again, then said, 'Only if you mean something like the corner of the carpet.'

'What surprised you about that?'

'It was scuffed and there was the cap of a bottle on it. When I picked that up, I found the carpet was wet so I used kitchen roll to dry it as best I could.'

'Have you any idea what the liquid was?'

'Not really. But it smelled a bit like drink.'

Gin that had spilled out of the neck of the bottle as it was forced into Vickers's mouth. 'You're being very helpful. What happened after you'd cleaned up in the sitting room?'

She'd taken the empty bottles, torn seals, and kitchen roll down to the kitchen and put them outside in the dustbin. She had returned upstairs to go along to ask the *señor* what he wanted for breakfast and had knocked on the bedroom door. Usually, he came to the door in a dressing gown and said whether it was for one or two, what he'd like and where he'd like it. But there'd been no answer. She'd called out. Then, unwillingly – who knew what might be going on? – she had opened the bedroom door and looked inside. The bed had not been slept in. Emboldened, she'd checked the bathroom and dressing-room and both had been empty. She'd returned downstairs by the front staircase and when part of the way down had seen ... had seen...

He told her how such sights always affected him so badly that he'd found the only thing to ease the shock was a drink. It might well help her. Would she like a reviving brandy, whisky, sherry?

'If Elena knew I had touched the *señor*'s drink...'

'If ever she complains, refer her to me and I will say I prescribed it. In any case, the *señor* can no longer enjoy his cellar, so it is a service to him not to allow it to be wasted.'

She finally admitted she would like a sherry.

He filled a schooner and handed this to her. To prevent her feeling any sense of guilt, he poured himself a large measure of Glenmorangie. He sat. The whisky was so velvety that his hitherto unassailable preference for *coñac* began to be assailed.

Once he was satisfied she had regained control of her emotions, he said, 'I think you were out last night?'

'What if I was?'

He smiled. 'Then I hope you had an enjoyable time. All that interests me is the time at which you returned to the staff cottage. I presume you were in a car?'

'Yes.'

'Elena says she heard...'

'She never stops prying into what I do.'

'I imagine she's only trying to protect you.'

'Protect me from what?'

'The kind of things from which young

ladies need protecting.'

'So what would she know about them? In any case, me and Mario weren't doing anything wrong.'

'I'm sure you weren't.'

'We went to a disco.'

'Elena heard a car at roughly eleven-thirty. Is that when you returned?'

She did not answer.

'When did you get back from the disco?'

She looked intently at the glass in her hand. 'What's it matter?'

'It is rather important.'

She drank. 'I suppose... I suppose it was around one.'

He supposed it had been well after one, but whatever the true time, her evidence made it clear that a car, which could not be accounted for, had driven past the staff cottage at around eleven-thirty. Which, allowing for time to talk and act, fitted in with Doctor Llabres's earliest estimated time of death. 'Tell me about Señor Vickers. What kind of person did you find him?'

'He was just...' She came to a stop.

'Was he a friendly man?'

'Not to the likes of us.'

'He was unfriendly to you?'

'I don't know how to say. When he first saw us each day, he never said good morning or asked how we were.'

'Some people don't come alive until after breakfast.'

'It wasn't really like that. Didn't matter whether he'd had or hadn't had his breakfast. We were different from him because he paid our wages. He walked higher.'

A not uncommon attitude of employers. All men might be born equal, but it was a stillborn equality.

'Was he difficult to work for?'

'He could be.'

'In what way?'

'Because sometimes he was so odd. Like if someone came to see him and he didn't know the name, we'd have to describe the person. He was that nervous, he'd go on and on at me because after dusting, I'd left one of the Lladro figures too close to the edge of the shelf and it might fall and break. Only it never was really that close because I made certain it wasn't. He could have a real temper.'

'What sort of thing would set that off?'

'Anything going wrong or not being as he wanted it to be. I remember the day he was shouting and there was a crash, so I rushed into the room to see what was wrong. The television, one of those big, flat ones, had failed as he watched some special English programme, so he'd picked up a stool and thrown it, knocked the set off its stand, and broken the screen. Of course, next day there was a new set with a bigger screen. When you've more money than there are stars, things don't go wrong for long.'

'Did anyone come and there was so fierce a row that he lost his temper?'

'Don't remember anything like that. There was just the phone call.'

'Tell me about it.'

'It was a man from Mahon. Spoke Spanish like any foreigner so it took time to understand he wanted to talk to the *señor*. When I told the *señor*, he was furious and for the rest of the day remained in a foul temper. I wasn't doing anything right; he told Elena she'd overcooked the meal. She swore she'd give in her notice, but didn't. She's always full of what she's going to do and never does.'

'What was the name of the man from Mahon?'

'Don't remember.'

'You say he was a foreigner – English?'

'Could have been.'

'How do you know where he was phoning from?'

'The phones here say what is the number at the other end. My cousin lives in Mahon, so I could tell.'

'Can you remember the number or any part of it?'

'No.'

'When was this?'

She thought. 'Couldn't be that long ago. Maybe around the end of last month. Just before he flew over there for the day.'

'To Menorca?'

'That's what I've just said.'

Alvarez's glass was empty. 'How are you feeling now? Would you like another drink?'

'Not for me.'

He wondered how odd it would appear if

in the circumstances he helped himself to another whisky. Rather odd, he regretfully decided. 'Elena mentioned the *señor* favoured the ladies.'

'I'll say he did. She kept on saying she couldn't go on working here because it was becoming a *casa de putas*. I told her it wasn't like that. In a *casa de putas*, it's a man hurrying to see a woman, here it was a woman hurrying to see him... She shouted that I shouldn't know about such things. She thinks I don't know anything.'

'One or two of his ladies were married, I believe. Can you give me some names?'

'You're like Elena. What's it to you what went on?'

'Because there's the possibility the *señor* did not die in an accident.'

'You aren't saying...'

'He may have been murdered.'

She began to shiver; her features became strained as she made a low moaning sound.

He stood. 'Give me your glass.'

Wordlessly, but not silently, she handed it to him.

He carried it, and his own glass – one did

not scorn opportunity – across to the cocktail cabinet, refilled both.

'Drink this quickly,' he said as he handed her the schooner.

Some of the sherry slopped over the edge of the glass as she raised it to her mouth. But it seemed his remedy for incipient hysterics worked, much to his relief since the only other cure he knew was a traditional slap on the face and as an inspector in the Cuerpo that was hardly to be recommended; should it ever become known what he had done, mean-minded opponents (to be found in the Guardia) might try to put the wrong interpretation on his action.

'To think that someone got into the house to ... to murder him,' she said, her voice shrill.

'As yet, that's only a possibility and I have to find out whether or not it's fact. You can help me do that and also, if it was not an accident, who might be the guilty person.'

'You don't think... You can't think...'

'As I said earlier, I am quite certain you know absolutely nothing about his death.' It occurred to him that an adverse reference to

Elena at this point might not be amiss. 'I was hoping Elena would help me, but she doesn't seem to be too keen to do so.'

'She wouldn't. Maybe she did it, because the *señor* twice told her that her cooking wasn't as brilliant as she thought.'

It was an absurd suggestion. Or was it? A cook of Elena's brilliance would possess endless pride in her skill and to denigrate that would be to insult her beyond measure; in the kitchen there would be many knives with edges razor sharp; a woman's tights were soft but strong; she probably possessed the strength to force Vickers up and over the balustrades...

'Still, I don't suppose she did,' Ana said regretfully. 'She's only good for shouting.'

He was glad Ana had restored a measure of common sense. 'Would you be able to judge which of the women who came here on their own were married?'

'Of course I would.'

'Even if she'd removed her wedding ring?'

'You think that makes a difference?'

He had always presumed it must. So what hidden sign identified a married woman to another woman? He decided not to ask. There were times when ignorance maintained peace of mind. 'Tell me about them.'

It became clear Ana had taken a fairly close interest in the visiting women. 'There's the blonde who gets the colour out of a bottle and dresses like her husband's blind.'

'Why do you suggest that?'

'Her clothes don't leave anything to wonder about.'

Surely one would have to employ a little imagination? 'What's her name?'

'Never heard it.'

'What more can you tell me about her?'

'Only that she arrived in a smart little soft-top car, they'd gallop upstairs, and it'd be a long time before they came downstairs. Likely she was so tired when she got back home, she told her husband she had a headache and went straight to bed.'

'The *señor* was lucky the headache would come after and not before.'

'What d'you mean?'

'Nothing.' It saddened him to have confirmed how casually a wife would betray her husband; women lacked any sense of loyalty. 'Have you an idea where she's from?'

'No.'

'She never said or did anything to suggest if she lived locally?'

'Don't think so.'

'You mentioned she had a soft-top car. What make is it?'

'Can't say. Likely Tollo can—'

'Tollo?'

'Diaz. He's always making out he knows everything about cars. My Mario's just the same. He scares me driving. I tell him, he's no Alonso.'

'What about other married women who came here on their own?'

She spoke unevenly, sometimes quickly, sometimes slowly as she tried to remember. There was Joan. Strange to hear a woman called Joan when it was a man's name. She seemed nicer than Susan, not that either could really be nice, warming another man's bed. Although, she added, one could maybe understand. The *señor* was so rich and handsome... Her voice trembled.

'Remember him like that.'

'But ... but I can't stop seeing him lying in

the hall.'

He feared hysterics again. As he refilled their glasses, he wondered if he could afford to drink Glenmorangie. Sanity returned. Could he afford to exchange his Ibiza for a Lamborghini?

It took time and an empty glass for her to continue. 'Then there's...' She tried to pronounce the name and failed.

Alvarez made several suggestions, which were rejected.

Whatever her name, she was like so many foreigners who seemed to find it difficult even to say good morning. Very obvious.

She had nothing more to tell him. He thanked her, asked her to contact him if she remembered anything more that might be useful, and said he'd have a word with Diaz. But when he looked at his watch, he found that if he were to return home in time for a drink before supper, he would have to choose between pursuing duty or pleasure.

Six

Alvarez only had time to regain his breath after climbing the stairs to his office when the telephone rang.

'The superior chief will speak to you,' announced the plum-voiced secretary autocratically.

There was a short pause before Salas said, 'Were all my inspectors as incapable of following an order as you, Alvarez, there would be chaos.'

'If, Señor, you are referring to—'

'There are so many orders you have ignored, you are incapable of distinguishing to which one I am now referring?'

'I just wanted to confirm the subject because sometimes we have a little difficulty in understanding each other.'

'There is no reason for your not understanding me; there is every reason for my
finding you largely incomprehensible.'

'Are you asking about my questioning of
Ana—'

'Who?'

'Ana, the maid at Ca Na Pantella.'

'Then would it not be an idea to identify
her?'

'I thought you'd remember.'

'Of course I remember; I'm not suffering
from the lack of attention which seems to
affect you.'

'But ... but if you remembered, why did
you ask?'

'Because I was trying to persuade you for
once to think long enough to make an intelligible report.'

'I still don't understand...'

'If we are to discuss what you do not
understand, neither of us will return home
this evening. Do you have a report to make?'

'Yes, Señor.'

'Then make it, without absurd and irrele-
vant comments.'

'When I had finished questioning Ana, I

decided it was too late to bother you with my report. As far as I could judge, she was still badly shocked and so I had to proceed slowly and carefully; even so, I found it somewhat confusing to follow all she said.'

'Yet perhaps less confusing than her task of understanding you.'

'She was not as helpful as I had hoped. However, she did confirm that Señor Vickers was very fond of the ladies.'

'Quite immaterial.'

'On the contrary, I think it is important.'

'Naturally, since you take an unwholesome interest in such matters.'

'Some of the women were married.'

'Then one can assume they were English.'

'A cuckolded husband has a very strong motive for committing murder.'

'But since Vickers may very well have suffered an accident, there is no need—'

'Señor, it was almost definitely murder.'

'Your reason for such certainty?'

'In part, the evidence Ana provided.'

'Because Vickers might possibly have given a husband cause to hate him...'

'There is much more than that.'

'A moment ago, you said her evidence was not as helpful as you had hoped. Yet now you wish to imply it was very helpful?'

'What I was referring to was the fact that she couldn't give me the names of any of the men.'

'What men?'

'The husbands of the married women who Señor Vickers entertained.'

'It has not occurred to you that they will bear the same name as their husbands?'

'She couldn't name any of them. However, there is the hope that Diaz will be able to give me the makes of cars...'

'Of what cars do you require the makes and why might the information be of the slightest importance? How many times do I have to complain about the chaotic reports you present? You will now collect your scattered thoughts, marshal the facts in chronological order, succinctly identify all those to whom you refer, and present a detailed, accurate review of your investigation.'

Alvarez did so.

'A man may prefer whisky to gin, but if none is available and he wishes to enjoy a drink, he will probably drink gin.'

'I checked the contents of the cocktail cabinet in the sitting room and there were three bottles of excellent malt whisky in it.'

'I am surprised.'

'You don't think it likely that if he enjoyed whisky, there would be some readily available?'

'The presence of the whisky was not what surprised me... Was there one or more dirty glasses in the room?'

'No.'

'Ana told you the corner of the carpet was scuffed and damp, she dried it as best she could, and there was a smell which she thought was alcoholic. And from those few facts, you try to deduce that the liquid was gin and had spilled out of a bottle as the neck was forced into Vickers's mouth. Have you had the liquid from the carpet analysed?'

'She used kitchen roll to soak it up which she threw away and then disinfected the whole area. There's nothing uncontaminated left to test.'

'Why?'

'How d'you mean, Señor?'

'You cannot appreciate her actions may have been a deliberate attempt to obscure any evidence?'

'I don't think that's feasible.'

'A good detective regards everything as feasible until he proves it is not.'

Then a good detective led a very busy life.

'And the two empty bottles?'

'Along with the paper, they were put in the recycling bins along the road and these had been emptied by the time I understood the need to check the bottles and paper.'

'Then there is not a scintilla of evidence to back up your proposition.'

'But what I suggest fits the sequence of events as we know them.'

'So once again, you make an assumption, then from that draw possibilities which you use to confirm the assumption.'

'One shouldn't forget the car.'

'You wish to suggest I would?'

'If Ana was not in the car which passed the staff cottage at around eleven-thirty, it was late for someone to be visiting the *señor* un-announced.'

'How do you know the visit was unexpected?'

'The staff had not been told, as was normal, to expect it.'

'Foreigners lead lives of such indolence, they lose all respect for time.'

'I suppose it could have been one of his married women who had had to wait for her husband to fall asleep after she had secretly fed him sleeping pills...'

'You will cease such unnatural and disgusting suppositions.'

'I think I mentioned another time that the front door key of Ca Na Pantella is missing. The murderer left the house, locked the door from the outside to make it seem that since there were no signs of a forced entry, there could not have been anyone else in the house that night. The fact that the alarm system was not set cannot be ignored, but apparently Vickers did forget to do this when he had been drinking heavily.'

'With your usual slackness, you have failed to tell me all this before. The possible significance is obvious, but that the facts have the significance you place on them is doubtful. Keys often go missing. You have just told me Vickers would sometimes forget to set the alarms.'

'It would be quite a coincidence for both things to happen at the same time by chance.'

'Coincidence is all too often used to draw together events that, in fact, have no connexion, yet it is taken to be an advantage if they had. Here, you are assuming a coincidence in order to support your assumption of murder.'

'Surely, coincidence or not, there now can be little doubt it was murder?'

'There can be considerable doubt.'

'Yet allowing for your doubt, Señor, while accepting for the moment that my assumption is possible, a man gained entrance into Ca Na Pantella obviously with Señor Vickers's permission. Since he is of a very nervous character, this means the visitor was well known to him. Of course, it could conceivably have been a woman since we are told we must accept sexual equality—'

'Refrain from such a ridiculous statement as that there is equality between man and woman. Women never were, never will be, the equal of men.'

'I do agree with that.'

'Your opinion in such matters is of no account.'

'So who was this visitor? To take the first possibility, he was the partner in a forth-coming S and M session...'

'One will not consider that.'

'But—'

'You do not understand me?'

'The second possibility is that the man inveigled his way into the house because he was a friend or acquaintance. Once inside, he used a knife to force the *señor* to allow his hands to be tied and to be taken upstairs to the sitting room where he was made to lie on the floor and gin was poured down his throat until he was drunk, a drunken man being many times more likely to fall over the balustrades in the gallery.

'The murderer hoped the death would be judged accidental, but was sharp enough to accept that a judgment of murder had to be a possibility. In which case, the most likely suspect would be a friend or acquaintance.

Since he was one or the other, he had to try to negate the obvious and he did this by using gin, not whisky; everyone who knew the *señor* at all well would be aware he did not like gin.'

There was a silence.

Salas broke it. 'Have you searched the house thoroughly?'

'Yes, Señor.'

'You have not reported doing so.'

'I thought it would be obvious when I said I did not find anything of immediate consequence apart from the question of razors and the lack of any signs of forced entry.'

'Is there a safe?'

'A small one in the sitting room of Vickers's suite.'

'Was there nothing of importance in it?'

'It's locked.'

'You find it exceptional that a safe should be locked?'

'Of course not.'

'You have called in a locksmith to open it?'

'Not yet.'

'A solution which escaped you?'

'I need an authorization from you, Señor.'

'You have asked me for this?'

'I was about to.'

'As you are always about to do a hundred and one things which should have been done long before. You will have the safe opened, examine the contents very carefully, and report to me immediately.'

'Yes, Señor.'

'Have you questioned the husbands of the married women who have visited Señor Vickers in circumstances in which they may be presumed to have committed adultery?'

'I have not yet been able to identify who they are.'

'Why not?'

'I have next to no facts to go on. Ana suggested one possible lead, but I have to speak to Diaz before I know if it is any good.'

'You have not spoken to him?'

'There hasn't been the time—'

'A competent detective makes time.'

'But surely this stage of the investigation must not be rushed? One does not wish our enquiries to make a husband start fearing his wife has been having an affair when she has not.'

'A possibility which cannot arise. It will always be obvious to a husband if his wife is betraying him.'

'I don't think so. In my experience—'

'I am not interested in your disgraceful incursions into a married woman's bed.'

'Señor, my experience is limited to cases which I have investigated. Quite often, I have known husbands who have been totally ignorant that their wives were having it off with other men.'

'You will identify those married women who visited the house on their own and establish which of their husbands may be considered a suspect should there be reason – legitimate reason – for accepting Vickers's death was not accidental. You will try to find the key to the front door of Ca Na Pantella. You say there is a garden. Every square centimetre of it will be searched.'

'But ... that could take days.'

'Not if the search is carried out diligently. Have you learned anything more about the phone call from Mahon which so enraged Vickers?'

'No.'

'You do not consider it a good idea to do so?'

'There just hasn't been the time...'

'How do you propose to identify the caller?'

It was not a question he had yet considered.

'Suppose you show sufficient initiative to speak to Telefonica and ask for details of Vickers's account?'

'It was an incoming call, so it will not be recorded.'

'A moment's thought might allow you to perceive that an incoming call which causes such emotion will probably provoke an outgoing call not long afterwards. Have you learned the contents of his will?'

'There's no copy of it loose, so it's probably in the safe.'

'Contact his solicitor and ask for details.'

'It could take a long time to track down which solicitor he used to draw up a will, so perhaps it would be better to wait to discover if it is in his safe.'

'Have you studied his bank accounts?'

'Like the will, I'm sure they're in the safe.'

'And will stay there unless I instruct you to find the time to bring in a locksmith to open it. Carry out my orders and report this evening.'

'This evening?'

'I did not make myself clear?'

'I'll do the best I can, but with such a heavy load of work—'

'A load which any of my other inspectors would not consider worth mentioning.' Salas rang off.

Alvarez slumped back in the chair. No one could do the impossible, yet that was what was now expected of him, no matter at what cost to himself. The quality of life was so easily destroyed.

'Had a busy morning?' Jaime asked, with the cheerfulness of one who had not.

Alvarez poured himself a large brandy, added ice. 'The superior chief is a slave driver.'

Dolores stepped through the bead curtain. No critic of style would have found words sufficiently dire to describe her appearance

– dishevelled midnight hair, smudges on her face, rolled up sleeves of a working dress which had long since passed maturity, strained apron with frayed edges – yet she carried herself so proudly she might have been clothed in ermine and silk. 'You are complaining about being overworked?'

'I'm having to do the work of three men.'

'Which will be less than that of one woman... Neither of you will drink any more.'

'But my glass is empty,' Jaime complained.

'Which is how it will remain. I am not cooking *Lomo de cerdo con salsa agridulce* to have it eaten by anyone unable to appreciate the hours of skilled work it has taken.'

Since Alvarez's glass was still half full, he was not as disturbed as he might have been by her demand of abstinence. And when she cooked this dish, the gods would spurn ambrosia for a taste of it. Despite everything, there were times when life *was* worth living.

Seven

'It's good soil.' Alvarez let the handful slither through his fingers and fall back on to the bed of roses.

'It should be with all the compost, peat, and horse dung I get from the stables up the road,' Diaz said.

'It would grow good vegetables.'

'As I told the *señor*, more than once. But foreigners throw their money away on lawns and flowers.' Diaz was squatly built, with very broad shoulders. His face had been leathered by wind, rain and sun; he always spoke Mallorquin because his grandfather had, due to politics, been shot during the Civil War and family bitterness had never lessened.

'If this were my place,' Alvarez said slowly,

82

'I'd maybe have a few flowers, but for the rest, I'd grow peppers, tomatoes, lettuces, aubergines, beans, carrots, cabbages, cauliflowers.' He looked across the garden, seeing the finca of his thoughts. 'And over there would be orange, lemon, pear, plum, grapefruit, and pomegranate trees.'

'But it ain't ever going to be yours to plant anything.'

'Maybe, but a man can dream.'

'A dream never filled a belly.'

'It would be a sadder world without them ... I'd like a word with you.'

'Ain't that what you've just been having?'

'About the *señor*, poor man.'

'Poor? With his money?'

'He's dead.'

'Then he ain't poor or rich.' Diaz always wanted authority to understand he wouldn't bow to it; however, he was careful never to be too openly antagonistic, remembering the fate of his grandfather.

'What did you think of him?'

'Who?'

Well aware that Diaz was considerably more intelligent than he was trying to make

83

out, Alvarez failed to express his annoyance as had been expected. He answered amiably: 'Was Señor Vickers a good employer?'

'There ain't no such thing.'

'Some are better than others.'

'And some are a bloody sight worse. I'd say good morning, he'd maybe bother to nod his head; I grow the finest roses on the island, but there wasn't never a word of praise from him.'

'The English are reserved.'

'You call it reserve? Soon after I started working here, I met him in the market when I was with the wife. Of course I introduced her, same as anyone would. So what did he do? Said "Hullo" like he was telling us both to bugger off, walked on. But in the market he wasn't no *señor* and I was better than him because when I'm introduced, I chat.'

'So you'd no reason to like him?'

'That's right.'

'I've been told he was fond of women?'

'Worse than a sixteen-year-old on the pull.'

'And some of the women were married?'

'A neighbour's peaches are always sweeter.'

'I'd like to know the names of the marrieds.'

'You think you would stand a chance?'

'I need to talk to them, that's all.'

'While lying down?'

'Come on, some names.'

'How am I supposed to know which ones are married?'

'The women in the kitchen say they can always tell.'

'You reckon that could be right?'

'I hope not. But they'll have gossiped and you'll have listened. And likely you've seen 'em arrive all nervous, hoping the husband doesn't suddenly drive up and find 'em at it.'

'I mind me own business.'

'Then you weren't born on the island. Have you seen the woman who drives a soft-top?'

Diaz scratched his right ear. 'How would I know?'

'By remembering.'

'What's it to you?'

'I've explained. I need a chat with those who are married.'

'Don't matter about the husbands? Not to blokes like you.'

'I'm no sadist, so I'll make it certain the husbands don't start worrying. So have you seen a woman come here in a soft-top?'

Diaz hawked and spat. 'Seen more of her than her husband should want.'

'So I heard.'

'Her clothes make a man start thinking.'

'I'd have thought it was her, not her clothes. What does she look like?'

'If she were in a tomato catalogue, she'd be round, firm, smooth, and full of flavour.'

'Only she's not a tomato.'

'More's the pity or you could pick her.'

'What make is her car?'

'Volkswagen.'

'The colour?'

'Silver.'

'New, middle-aged, old?'

'Newish.'

'What's the registration number?'

'Why would I know that?'

'The letters might have caught and held

your interest because they were the initials of a friend; the numbers could have meant something to you.'

'They didn't.'

'Can you tell me anything more about her?'

'No.'

'So move on to the next married.'

Diaz used thumb and forefinger to dead-head a rose. He straightened up. 'There's one with a Volvo estate; bulky, but stylish.'

'She's fat?'

'I'm talking about the car.'

'Keep with the woman.'

'Looks like she's just spent a fortune at a beauty place. The kind of woman who demands you take a shower first.'

'What colour is the Volvo?'

'Thought you wanted to stay with the women?'

'Move on to the car.'

'Blue.'

'Newish.'

'Out of the factory in the last couple of months.'

'Registration number?'

'You think I'm in security?'

'What other women can you remember?'

'There's one comes along more often than any of the others. Always has a chat if she sees me.'

'She speaks good Spanish?'

'A sight better than the *señor* did.'

'Did you learn her name?'

'No.'

'Forget tomatoes and tell me what she looks like.'

'Not bad-looking, but nothing to get the blood rising. The kind you meet; the others you only see on the telly or in *¡Hola!*.'

'What's her car?'

'A yellow Clio that needs pensioning off.'

'You know the number?'

Diaz did not bother to answer.

'Is that the lot?'

'No. There's the Smart car, black and white.'

'What make?'

'I've just told you.'

'I thought you meant a posh car.'

'Seems like one has to explain everything twice to blokes like you.'

'And the woman?'

'She'd have you panting. Your fantasies come to life.'

'Is that all?'

'Aren't you ever satisfied?'

'I'm talking about women.'

'So am I. That's the lot, so can I get back to work?'

'If you want to.'

'That surprises you?'

In the face of the insult, Alvarez did not thank Diaz for his help. He turned to leave.

'Hang on,' Diaz said. 'I've just remembered another.'

'Tell me.'

'A red Mercedes.'

'What's the woman like?'

'You'd have her if you'd just won El Gordo and had the money for the best of everything. But a couple of times, I've seen a man driving.'

If a man suspected his wife, he was likely to try to learn whether his suspicions were justified.

Back in the office, Alvarez phoned Telefonica and asked for a printout of Vickers's telephone account over the past three months. First this was impossible; then perhaps it could be done when the over-worked staff had the time; finally, after a reference to Salas's authority, it would be sent as soon as possible.

He phoned the leading locksmith in Palma. Nothing could be done for the moment as one of the employees was on holiday and the pressure of work... The superior chief could shout as much as he liked, but unless he liked to force the safe himself, he was going to have to wait. Alvarez mentioned a rumour he had recently heard. One of their employees was also working for himself in a way that would bring severe discredit to the firm... Of course that was absolute nonsense. A rumour like that could ruin the firm's integrity. If Inspector Alvarez would attest there was not a word of truth in the malicious rumour, perhaps someone could very soon be found to open the safe at Ca Na Pantella...

He phoned several banks and finally learned at which one the dead man had had two accounts. But no details of either account could or would be given without an authorized request, issued by a senior member of the Cuerpo. Yes, the speaker had been at school with Alvarez and he did remember the time when Alvarez had saved him from severe punishment... Perhaps a short, spoken précis would not break the rules, as must any written one.

Feeling as if he had become a call-centre slave, he phoned Vehicles and explained he wanted a list of the owners of certain cars and their addresses. The registration numbers? Regretfully, he could not supply any.

Vehicles became scornfully angry. Was Alvarez living in a parallel world? Had no one bothered to tell him there were tens of thousands, hundreds of thousands, of each model on the roads...? The computer? He believed a computer would make the job as easy as shelling peas? Then he knew as much about computers as catching moonbeams. And it didn't matter what his superior chief said... The director general had expressed his interest in the case? Perhaps...

He returned the receiver to its cradle. Most problems could be solved with the help of nostalgia, lies, threats, blackmail, or murder. He relaxed.

The door was flung open and one of the *cabos* entered, several sheets of paper in his right hand. 'Having your siesta at work?'

'Thinking.'

'Sounds very unlikely. This has just come through on the fax.' He dropped the papers on to the desk. 'Have a good think,' he said before he left.

Alvarez stared at the papers the *cabo* had left and was gloomily certain, because of their prolixity, they had come from the superior chief. Further orders detailing an inspector's duties and how these were to be carried out; more demands for reports on this and that; a posting to furthest Extremadura...?

To his astonishment, there were lists of Vickers's telephone calls over the past months. If Telefonica could become so efficient, where would the changes end?

The majority of calls were local; a lesser

number were to England and Jersey and almost as many to Menorca. He looked at his watch, came quickly to his feet. He was late for his *merienda*.

The old square, stiflingly hot, was filled with tourists who sat and drank at the tables set outside the cafés. Benito Dominguez had written that nothing was more invigorating than to sit and drink at leisure. Lucky the man who had the chance.

He entered Bar Llueso, went up to the bar.

'What's it to be?' the bartender asked. 'A Coke Light? I'm bored with life and longing for something impossible to happen.'

'Stop longing and give me the usual.'

'Life was never meant to be this stolid.' He turned away, filled a holder with ground coffee and fitted it into the espresso machine, picked up a bottle of Soberano and poured a drink, put the glass down on the counter.

Alvarez stared at the glass. 'Are you suffering from cramp in the right hand?'

'It's the boss.'

'What's he to do with half measures?'

'Says the bar's not making the money it should because I'm too generous.'

'Then he never drinks here.'

'Are you suggesting I've ever given you small measure?'

'What do you call this?' Alvarez pointed at the glass.

'That's the measure I've been told to serve.'

'Forget the crap and pour me a decent *coñac*.'

'You want me fired?'

'I want a drink.'

'One day you'll get your just desserts,' the bartender muttered as he poured more brandy into the glass. He went down the counter to serve another customer.

Alvarez drank some brandy, poured the rest into the coffee and, to save time, indicated he'd want a refill. Unwillingly, his thoughts turned to work. Were Vickers's phone calls likely to be of any consequence? Probably most of them were to women. The call to Mahon which had provoked so notable a rage, mentioned by Ana, was probably telling him enough was enough and get lost. But if one woman rejected his advances, there were many ready to accept them. The world's pleasures were for the rich.

The bartender walked up to where he sat. 'You look like life's turned extra sour.'

'It can be so unfair.'

'Stand on my side of the bar and you'll learn it's never anything else.'

Alvarez lit a cigarette. Despite the overwhelming pressure of work from the Vickers case, he had to produce that report concerning the previous month's work and fax 'the copy' to the superior chief to prove that the original had been sent several days previously. He searched for any notes he might have made and failed to find one. This meant he would have to try and remember details and when he could not, use imagination.

He picked up the list of phone calls made by Vickers and dialled the number in Mahon. There was no answer. He waited a few moments, dialled again. No answer. There seemed little point in trying again until the next day, so he relaxed.

Eight

Alvarez stared at the fax which had just been handed to him. Page after page of names and addresses. What a start to a Saturday! Gone was the pleasure of a calm weekend. In their resentment at having to compile the list, were Vehicles making a fool of him? Were they laughing at the thought of his trying to question so many people?

He regained a measure of calm. Remember those words of wisdom. A mountain in the mind may be but a hillock on the ground. If he assumed the woman who drove the car lived locally, since she frequently visited Vickers (forget Salas's disapproval of assumptions), that she was not Mallorquin or Spanish, since no decent woman would behave so appallingly, then the numbers could be greatly reduced.

Forty minutes later, four names remained. He checked the time. Two hours to lunch (Dolores had been in an unusually good mood earlier so she might be cooking one of her special dishes) and so there was time to drive to the first address on the list. Yet foreigners ate earlier than was the local custom and it was bad manners to interrupt a meal. It would be better to leave things until the afternoon; late afternoon since he always had a prolonged siesta on a Saturday and a Sunday.

The block of flats was three roads back from the front in Port Llueso and name tabs of the security call system showed that the Kerrs lived on the fourth floor. He pressed that button and after a few seconds a male voice, difficult to hear through the crackles, asked in English: 'Who is it?'

'Inspector Alvarez, Cuerpo General de Policia.'

'How's that?'

He repeated his name.

'What d'you want?'

'To speak to you, Señor.'

'Why?'

'If I may meet you in your flat, I will tell you.'

The door lock buzzed and he went into the small foyer which seemed much larger than it actually was because it was lined with mirrors. He was thankful there was a lift, saving the need to climb four flights of stairs.

On the fourth floor, the front door of the flat to the right was open and a man stood in the doorway.

'Señor Kerr?'

'That's me.'

Kerr was of medium height and well built; both his attitude and speech were antagonistic.

'I am sorry to bother you,' Alvarez said politely.

'So why are you?'

'I will explain.'

'You want to come in?'

'It would be more comfortable than standing here.' Alvarez smiled.

Kerr hesitated long enough to prevent any

suggestion of welcome, finally stood to one side to allow Alvarez to enter. He led the way into an oblong sitting room, over-furnished, with French windows at the far end which gave access to a small balcony on which sat a patio table and chairs.

Kerr stood in the centre of the room. 'So what's this all about?' he demanded.

'I understand you own a red Mercedes saloon car.'

'And if I do?'

'You may be able to help us. Two days ago, at about midday, there was a serious road accident on the old Llueso–Playa Neuva road. A Renault came round a corner, skidded, and went straight into an oncoming Fiesta, the driver of which was badly injured. The driver of the Renault denies he was speeding and claims there was something on the road, he suggests oil, which caused him to lose control. The traffic police found no trace of oil, or anything of a similar nature, on the road. They talked to a man who had been working in a nearby field; he saw the crash and he says that shortly before it, a red Mercedes had driven past without any sign of trouble. So I'm sure you'll understand that we should very much like to talk to the driver of the Mercedes to find out if he noticed anything unusual about the road.'

'Why think that car was mine?'

'I am here because you own that make of car, Señor, not because I have any indication it was yours. It is our only way of finding the driver.'

'I haven't been on that road in a month of Sundays; no call to go on it.'

'Are you married?'

'What the devil has that to do with it?'

'Might your wife have been driving your car that day?'

'How the hell am I supposed to remember? But she'd no more reason to be there than I had.'

'Nevertheless, I should like to speak to her.'

'Why?'

'To ask her if she was driving on that road that day.'

'I've just told you.'

'Naturally, I accept what you have said,

but I have to speak to anyone who might have been driving your car that day. Is she here?'

'She's down at the shops.'

'Then perhaps I may call back another time to ask her to make a statement.'

'A waste of bloody time.'

'I fear we often have to waste other people's time as well as our own.' He added that this was a sad time for the English community. He'd been told what a charming man Señor Vickers had been...

'Whoever told you that must have had his nose too close. Vickers was a jumped-up barrow-boy with the morals of an alley cat. Ten to one, he swindled his way to the money.'

Kerr had spoken with considerable anger. The anger of a husband for his wife's seducer? 'I will not trouble you any more, Señor; that is, until I return to have a word with your wife.'

Kerr said nothing. Alvarez walked out of the sitting room into the hall; as he did so, the front door was opened and Kerr's wife entered, a shopping bag in one hand.

She stared at him, then beyond him at her husband.

'He's a policeman,' Kerr muttered, in answer to the unasked question.

'What's the trouble?' She was short, plump and, inadvisably, wore a tight blouse and slacks. Her features were of the kind which had once adorned Soviet posters proclaiming the joys of labouring for the glory of the state.

'He's been asking questions about a car crash and says he's got to do the same with you.'

'Why?'

'I am happy to say, Señora, that it will no longer be necessary to trouble you,' Alvarez assured her.

'Why not?' demanded Kerr.

Because his wife would not have tempted a second Crusoe. 'What you have told me, Señor, means I do not have to trouble her.'

'I haven't said anything since you demanded to speak to her.'

'You have been very helpful. Thank you, Señor.'

Minutes later, as he sat behind the wheel

of his car, he wondered what might be the cause of Kerr's obvious hatred of Vickers. Wealth? Yet the Kerrs seemed to enjoy a pleasant, comfortable standard of living. Still, few were content with what they had, and envied those who had more. Envy and hate were bedfellows; or perhaps, with such a wife, Kerr's envy had not been directed at Vickers's wealth, but at his lifestyle.

Alvarez looked at his watch, tried to convince himself that what was left of his working morning was too short to continue working. He failed. Still, at least Mrs Sewell lived in the village which meant it would not take him long to return home. And Diaz's description of her had painted a second Diana, risen from the sea.

She lived in one of the terrace houses in Carrer de Cardenal Rossell; recently, the outer rendering of Mallorquin cement had been chipped away on the road side to reveal the original rock wall, restoring character. The foreigners were responsible for many changes, some bad, some good and one of these was to teach the ordinary Mallorquins to have pride in their properties.

Because the owner was a foreigner, Alvarez did not enter the *entrada* and call out, but knocked and waited. The panelled wooden door was opened and he introduced himself to a woman in her late sixties or early seventies, carefully made-up and dressed casually, but with obvious care.

'A detective? That's exciting!' she said cheerfully.

'Is Señora Sewell here?'

'Indeed, she is. You are talking to her... You are surprised?'

So much for Diaz's description! He would find a way of subtly getting his own back.

'I do not need to bother you further, Señora, and apologize for having done so.'

She studied him for several seconds before she said: 'You ask for me by name, so you came here to speak to me, yet having met me, you no longer wish to do so?'

'There has been a slight mistake.'

'I've been on my own all day and would enjoy talking to someone, so you can come in and have a drink and explain what mistake appeared to incriminate me.'

'You are very kind, Señora, but I must—'

'I insist!'

She had spoken lightly, but he had not missed the note of appeal. He followed her into the sitting room, once two small rooms (in the front one, a mule had probably been kept) and now, with the aid of an RSJ, stretched from front to back of the house. Through the back window a small patio, in the centre of which grew an orange tree, was visible.

He sat on a comfortable chair, said that he would like a *coñac* with just ice.

'The favourite drink of my husband.' She noticed his expression. 'He died three years ago, just weeks before the builders finished altering this house.'

There had been a slight catch in her voice. A woman of considerable emotion, he judged, who tried to keep that hidden.

She handed him a glass, settled on the small settee. 'Now, explain why you bothered to come here to speak to me, met me, and decided you did not wish to talk to me after all?'

She reminded him of a distant cousin; as

small as a sparrow, sharp as an eagle. He told her about the mythical car crash and why he was trying to identify the driver of the other car.

'I'm surprised, since it was that serious, that it hasn't been reported in the papers.'

'I expect it was in the local Spanish ones.'

'Then I must have missed reading about it. I have a Spanish newspaper every day to try to improve my Castilian. I know I should be trying to learn Mallorquin since one should always speak the language of where one lives, but I'm too old. And in any case – I hope you won't mind my saying this – I don't find it a very attractive-sounding language, maybe because it is so often spoken very loudly... Have you learned how the injured person is?'

'His injuries are not as serious as first suspected.'

'I am glad. Where exactly did it happen on the old Llueso–Palma Neuva road? Near that very sharp corner at the bridge over the *torrente*?'

'It was beyond another corner, which wasn't very sharp, which was why the driver was probably driving too quickly.' Safer not to be more specific.

'And you obviously thought I might have been driving along that road in my little Smart car just before the crash. But you haven't asked me if I was.'

'The driver was probably a man.'

'You knew I was a woman before you came here.'

'Eyewitnesses can seldom be believed implicitly.'

'Yet you still haven't asked me. Perhaps you have not mentioned everything? Still, I can assure you it was not I who was driving on that road on the day in question.'

He left twenty minutes later, having promised to return when he had the time. Once in his car, he realized he had forgotten to ask her what she thought of Vickers in order to help him gain a rounded picture of the victim. Still, there could be little doubt what the tenor of her answer would have been.

On his return to Llueso, he phoned Mahon. Yet again, there was no reply. He spoke to the Menorquin Cuerpo and asked for someone to go along to the address and learn where the owner was. His request was met with a bitter question: Hadn't anyone told him it was Saturday? He replied that in Mallorca, all days of the week were the same.

Alvarez sat at the dining-room table and poured himself a drink.

'I've had the boss on my back all day,' Jaime complained. 'I expect the wife has been giving him hell. According to Lucía, she's a typical cow...' He stopped abruptly. 'Good job she didn't hear me say that.'

'Hear you say what?' came the call from the kitchen.

'Telling me you've been working so hard we must be about to enjoy a feast,' Alvarez hastily called back, knowing Jaime would not readily answer.

She looked through the bead curtain. 'It is unusual to find that my husband considers the amount of work I do.' She turned her head to face Jaime. 'Why did you not wish me to hear words which would have been welcome?'

'He thought you wanted the meal to be a

complete surprise,' Alvarez said.

'Words slide easily over a smooth tongue.' She withdrew into the kitchen.

The phone rang. Neither Alvarez nor Jaime immediately moved, expecting Dolores to answer the call. She did not.

'It won't be for me,' Jaime said.

Which was probably true, Alvarez acknowledged as he reluctantly stood. He went through to the *entrada*, answered the call.

'Is that you, Enrique?'

He identified the caller as one of the *cabos*. 'That seems possible since this is where I live.'

'Where have you been all morning?'

'Working.'

'That joke has whiskers on it. Señor Perez has tried to phone you several times and became furious when told you're on holiday.'

'I don't know a Perez.'

'You told him you wanted a safe forced open and it was so important it had to be done yesterday. With great effort and much rearranging of schedules, he detailed someone to do the work, yet now can't get hold of you to say where and exactly when. Small wonder he's furious.'

He had forgotten about the safe. 'Phone him back and say I'm sorry, I've been tied up in a major case and I'll be in touch first thing tomorrow... I mean, Monday.'

'You can do that.'

'When I don't know the number?'

'Then how did you phone him in the first place?'

'By telepathy,' he answered.

He returned to the sitting room, sat, lifted his glass and drained it.

'The boss has been giving me hell,' Jaime complained.

'So you said.'

'Don't try to appear sympathetic, will you?'

'If you had all my problems to cope with, you wouldn't need sympathy, you'd need a lifeboat.'

Nine

Sunday was a day of rest. Unless one's superior chief was Salas, a man so fuelled with suspicion he might check up whether he – Alvarez – was pursuing the case as, in his opinion, any competent inspector should and would be.

Once in his office, Alvarez dialled the number in Mahon. It was not answered. Should he contact the Cuerpo there again? To do so might cause them to complain; it was better left. He tried to find some – any – notes which would enable him to write that report for Salas, but failed. The day was hot, the room stuffy, and the pleasure of being out in the open not to be foregone. He would question the Cutlers.

Ca'n Afortunato was a large house with a

view of the bay, the mountains, and Santa Antonia on top of Puig Antonia, once the home of a hermit reputed to have lived there for seventy-six years; now the rock-built buildings were looked after by nuns.

He parked in front of a double garage in which were a VW soft-top and a black Jaguar. As he stepped out of his car, a pair of giant schnauzers raced around the corner of the house, came to a stop a couple of metres from him, barked several times before regarding him with open mouths and large teeth. He stood very still as he tried to work out whether he could jump back into his car and slam the door shut before providing them with a feast.

'They're quite safe,' a woman called out in Mallorquin.

Had anyone told them that? Standing in the front porch, three steps above ground level, was a middle-aged woman who wore an apron over her clothes.

'They're trained guard dogs.'

More like canine tanks. 'I am Inspector Alvarez of the Cuerpo General de Policia.'

She spoke with sharp annoyance. 'You

think you have to tell me that?'

Clearly, he should know who she was, but before he looked back at her he made certain the dogs were not advancing. Freed from the fear of dismemberment, he now unfortunately identified her as one of Dolores's friends. Unfortunately because if she mentioned that he had not recognized her, Dolores would be annoyed and would not listen to his plea that his mind had been severely distracted. 'Of course not, Matilde. It was just my fun.'

'A strange sort of joke! Are you going to keep standing there?'

'Until they allow me to move.' He pointed at the two dogs.

'What are you scared of? They won't hurt anyone unless told to.'

So long as they weren't hungry? He carefully walked forward, climbed the steps to the patio. He looked out across the flat land to the distant bay. 'You'd have to look very hard to find somewhere more beautiful to live.'

'Money always knows where to go,' she said.

'The Cutlers are rich?'

'You think they live here yet need to search their pockets for *centimos*?'

An employee was often the best judge of the character of an employer and, since they were speaking in Mallorquin, they were unlikely to be understood if anyone overheard them. 'How do you find them?'

'I do my work, they pay me.'

'Are they friendly?'

'As friendly as a block of ice.'

'I've been told the *señora* is attractive.'

'A man will say so. As for me, if she confessed she was a *puta*, I would not be surprised.'

'Why's that?'

'She walks around showing much of what a woman should hide.'

'Doesn't the *señor* object?'

'When an old ram fancies a young ewe, it's the ewe decides on the tupping.'

'She wanders?'

'Of course.'

'Have you ever seen an Englishman called Vickers here?'

'The one who died in an accident?'

'That's him.'

'So it's because of the dead man you're asking questions?'

'Not really.'

'Then what's it matter if he's been here?'

'I'd just like to know.'

She was silent for a moment, then said: 'He turned up more often than the *señor* liked.'

'What makes you say that?'

'Because I've eyes and ears.'

'So what have your eyes seen and your ears heard?'

'I understand little English, but it was not necessary to do so after Señor Vickers had been here and the *señor* was shouting his head off, the *señora* all weepy.'

'That happened often?'

'Often enough.'

'How did it end?'

'She got him up to bed.'

'You think she and Señor Vickers were having it off together?'

'Of course I do. He looked at her, she looked at him and the air between them boiled. And there's no surprise there, with him as handsome as they come and even richer than the *señor*.'

'Ever tempted?'

'Another strange joke?' she said furiously. 'I am not a foreign woman.'

Dolores would hear about this and demand how he could have been so crudely stupid as to suggest, even in fun, that she would misbehave. He tried to think of a way to lessen the offence, but failed. He took the coward's route. 'I'd better have a word with the *señor* now.'

She sniffed with loud significance as she moved to one side to let him enter. He followed her through the house and out to the main patio and the large kidney-shaped pool in which a man and a woman were swimming.

'Inspector Alvarez,' Matilde announced, her tone still expressing anger.

Cutler, in the shallow end, stood. Pamela continued to swim with a stylish crawl. Alvarez chanced to notice she was wearing a monokini.

'What's the problem?' Cutler asked.

Nearer sixty-five than fifty-five, Alvarez

judged. The hard-featured face of a man who was used to giving orders and having them obeyed; a thickset body, well muscled. 'I should like to ask a few questions, Señor.'

'What about?'

Cutler was not bothering to be polite and welcoming as most Mallorquins would, whatever the reason for the visit. 'I am making enquiries concerning a motor crash. Do you own a silver soft-top Volkswagen?'

'No.'

'Does the *señora*?'

'Yes.'

'Then you and she may be able to help me.'

'This is nonsense! I'm not having you crashing about here on a Sunday. Come back another day.'

'Don't you think...' Pamela began as she swam back towards the shallow end.

'No, I don't.'

'Come on, sweetie, lighten up.'

'He can come back at a time convenient to us.'

'But we don't know why he's here.'

'You heard; it's to do with a car crash. We

haven't been in one.'

'But there must be a better reason for him wanting us to help. Let's sit on the patio and have a drink while he tells us what it is.'

'It's too early to drink.'

'Don't you often say it's never too early?' She spoke in a soft voice with bantering affection. She took hold of his hand as she looked up. 'You will have a drink with us, won't you, Inspector?'

'That would be very pleasant, Señora.'

She climbed out of the pool, followed by her husband. Diaz had failed to be sufficiently complimentary. She would charm Simeon Stylites off his pillar. An oval, unlined face, blonde curly hair, deep blue eyes, a chirpy, *retroussé* nose, full, generous lips, breasts a perfection of human art...

'Shall we sit on the patio?' she asked.

'If you want,' Cutler muttered.

Alvarez and Cutler sat; she remained standing.

'I can offer you anything you'd like, Inspector, so what would you?' she said.

Not a question to put to him when twin arcadian, rose-tipped hillocks were within centimetres of his face. 'May I have a *coñac* with just ice, please?'

'Keith?'

'I don't want anything.'

She stepped across to her husband, put her arms around his neck and leaned her breasts against his shoulder. 'Come on, love, how about I get you some champagne?'

He muttered his agreement.

She went indoors.

'What's all this about a car crash?' Cutler demanded.

'There was a serious road crash on the Llueso–Palma Neuva road...' Alvarez had told the story twice before and familiarity had the effect of momentarily making him think he might be speaking the truth.

'I wasn't anywhere near that road,' Cutler snapped.

'And the *señora*?'

'Neither of us was.'

'I trust you won't object if I ask her to confirm that?'

'Of course I bloody well will. I object to being called a liar.'

'I am not doing so, Señor. My reason for

119

wishing to speak to her is that we have to obtain best evidence, which means evidence given by the person concerned.'

'You think I don't know what she gets up to?'

'If so, Señor, you are a very fortunate or unfortunate husband.'

'Is that trying to be smart?'

'I'm sorry, my mind had wandered a little and I was remembering the old Mallorquin story about the lord who loved his wife so deeply that when he had to travel without her, he thought he would die from misery. Do you know it?'

'Never heard of it.'

'It's a very worrying story if one thinks about it.'

'Then forget it.'

'One day, in a pine forest, the lord came upon a net set between trees by a farmer, and in this was caught a nightingale. The lord, who loved to hear the beauty of a nightingale's song, released the bird which flew up on to a branch from where she spoke to him in words of golden cadences. Because he had released and not killed and eaten her, as the farmer would have done, he was granted one wish. The lord said that each night he was away from his beloved wife's side, he wished to be able to gaze on her and know that nothing bad had befallen her. The nightingale flew off. He continued on his way with his retinue of armed soldiers and that night, after he had eaten, he lay by the dying fire wrapped in his fur-lined coat, and suffered a wave of love and of despair at being on his own. He decided to learn if the nightingale had been speaking truly and wished himself back in his castle. He saw his wife in their bedchamber, but not alone. Thereafter, he killed every nightingale he saw.'

'You've come here to tell fairy stories?'

Pamela, who had changed into a frock which, to eager eyes, appeared to display more than it actually did, stepped through the opened doorway on to the patio, a tray in her hands. 'Have you been telling fairy stories, Inspector?' She passed a glass to Alvarez.

'He's been talking a load of crap.' Cutler brought the bottle out of the ice bucket, stripped off the foil, unwound the wire cage, held the cork and eased the bottle around it.

He filled the two glasses, handed one to her, drank deeply.

'Come on, Inspector,' she said, 'tell me what it was about. A beautiful princess and an ugly toad?'

'A nobleman who freed a nightingale and was rewarded with one wish.'

'What did he choose? A beautiful wife?'

'He already had one and loved her so much that he wanted to be able to see her and know she was all right when he was far from home. Unfortunately, the first time he enjoyed his wish, he found she was not alone.' He drank. He would have hoped for better quality brandy; this was similar to what he drank at home.

She looked at him, saw he was regarding her, hurriedly looked away. 'You call that a fairy story when it ends so nastily?'

'It was your husband who called it that.'

She fiddled with her glass. 'You haven't explained about the car crash.'

'I told him it was nothing to do with us,' Cutler snapped. 'But my word isn't good enough and he's got to ask you.'

'No, Señor,' Alvarez corrected, 'as I explained, I must ask the *señora* because I have to obtain best evidence which means hearing the facts from her, as she was directly involved.'

'Neither of us were bloody well involved.'

'You must blame my English. I meant I have to speak to the person who is best qualified to answer my question. Since I must ask if it was the *señora*'s car, she is the person to answer.'

'To answer what?' she asked.

For the fourth time, he described the fictional road crash.

'It certainly wasn't my car.'

'Thank you, Señora.'

'Is that all?'

'For the moment.'

'What the hell more can you want to know?' Cutler asked furiously.

'One can never tell where a case will lead, Señor, so I never promise a witness I will not be back.'

'If we weren't there, we can't goddamn know what the road was like.'

'Indeed, Señor. Now I will leave and not bother you again this Sunday.'

'I'll see you away,' Pamela said.

'He can find his own way,' Cutler snapped.

She led the way into the hall as Matilde stepped through another doorway. 'It's all right,' she said sharply.

Matilde returned inside, shut the door with more force than was necessary.

Pamela said, 'Were you... I mean ... that story...'

'Yes, Señora?'

'It doesn't matter.' She opened the door.

He said goodbye, she mumbled a response.

He was halfway to his car when the two giant schnauzers reappeared, looking even more daunting than before. Where was Matilde? Why didn't the *señora* come out to rescue him? Was this a deliberate attempt to silence him? There had recently been a programme on the television in which some ridiculously intrepid hunter had claimed that if one came face to face with a dangerous animal and was unarmed, the safest thing to do was move very slowly, showing no sense of panic, to the nearest point of safety; prey was expected to flee at speed and to see a potential victim moving slowly caused mental confusion...

He moved very slowly, reached his car, opened the driving door, got inside, slammed the door shut, more quickly than he had done anything in years. The dogs stared at him with annoyed regret. Deprived of their Sunday lunch.

Ten

Alvarez settled behind his desk and stared through the window at the sun-blasted wall of the house on the opposite side of the street. Monday. Days and days until midday Saturday and rest. Yet what rest had he enjoyed over the past weekend?

The phone rang.

'This is Inspector Cerda, Mahon. You wanted us to find out why no one was responding to the telephone calls you made. We determined the address was fifteen Carrer de Numanica and a policia was sent along. Señor Upton was found to be dead.'

Alvarez swore. 'I was hoping he would be able to help us in a very difficult case.'

'Then you're out of luck.'

The Menorquins were known to be self-

126

centred and unconcerned with the problems of others. 'What was it – a heart attack?'

'He fell downstairs, probably when drunk, and smacked his head on the corner of a table.'

'Good God!'

'Why the surprise? You don't get drunken accidents on your island?'

'How long has he been dead?'

'According to the doc, between four and five days.'

'Has there been a P.M.?'

'Later.'

'So what makes you say he was drunk?'

'When we see empty cans everywhere, we reckon he wasn't using the beer to wash with.'

'Were there any small cuts on his neck, under his chin?'

'No idea.'

'You didn't check the body?'

'The doctor said the Englishman had fallen and that was the cause of death. We're not here to question his decision.'

'Was his mouth damaged? Were there signs his wrists had been bound together?'

'What's the problem? I'm telling you, he drank, got tight, fell, smashed up his head, died, end of story.'

'I think you need to examine the body more closely.'

'Will it surprise you to learn I'm not interested in what you think?'

'It's virtually certain it wasn't an accident; it was murder.'

'You didn't know who lived at the address, you didn't know he was dead until I told you, you've not been within a hundred kilometres of here, yet you know it was murder.'

'Because of what happened here.'

'And I know it was an accident because of what happened here.' Cerda rang off.

Alvarez replaced the receiver. The Menorquins were so self-satisfied they'd never listen to anyone else. He drummed his fingers on the desk. Did he accept the verdict of accident? When there had to be a connexion between the two deaths because of all the phone calls, the drunken nature of the deaths, when Upton's death surely had to confirm Vickers's murder?

★ ★ ★

When he returned from his *merienda*, it was to be told that Salas wished to speak to him.

'What the devil have you been doing?'

He was dismayed by the anger with which Salas had spoken. 'I haven't been doing anything, Señor.'

'Normally, that is quite true. In this case, unfortunately, it is not. Are you incapable of appreciating the harm you have caused by your insulting behaviour?'

'My what?'

'You need to be told what is an insult or is normal social behaviour beyond your ken?'

'I haven't insulted anyone.'

'You would not imagine that a very competent member of the Cuerpo would consider it an insult to be called incompetent?'

'I haven't called anyone incompetent.'

'Superior Chief Calafat has made it very clear – I have to say, regrettably in terms stronger than necessary – that you have insulted him.'

'But I've never met or spoken to him.'

'Clearly, I need to explain something which I had mistakenly believed every member under my command understood and appreciated. When one has pride in one's command, an insult to any member of the team is an insult to oneself.'

'I would have thought that's taking things too far.'

'I did not ask for your opinion.'

'But if someone insults me, would you feel insulted?'

'The question is of no consequence since I am unable to have any pride in the command of a team of which you are a member.'

'How am I supposed to have insulted the superior chief?'

'You insulted Inspector Cerda.'

'I tried very hard to help him.'

'By accusing him of incompetence?'

'I pointed out why he was almost certainly wrong in his initial judgment.'

'He conducts an efficient investigation and reaches the conclusion that death was due to an accident. You, having conducted no investigation and with no knowledge of the facts, inform him he is wrong. That is your idea of helping him?'

'I would have explained why I said what I did, but he rang off.'

'No one can blame him for doing that.'

'I would have pointed out there must have been some connection between Vickers and Upton because of the many phone calls; that both men had been drunk when they fell; that the classic way of concealing murder is to fake an accident.'

'And I don't doubt you are about to say that if one assumes Vickers was murdered, the similarities in their deaths proves Upton was murdered and therefore there is the final proof that Vickers was murdered also?'

'It's more than just an assumption that Vickers was murdered.'

'Without proof, there is only assumption.'

'The phone calls to Upton in Mahon—'

'Are undeniable. What can and should be denied at this moment is that they play any part in the cases other than coincidence.'

'Señor, you have often said one should never rely on coincidence to prove an assertion.'

'There is not the same objection to using a coincidence to disprove something.'

'I am not certain I can appreciate the difference.'

'You do not surprise me. As soon as I ring off, you will phone Superior Chief Calafat in Mahon and will apologize for your insolent behaviour.'

'But I don't see why...' But the line was dead. He replaced the receiver, leaned over to open the right-hand drawer of the desk and brought out a bottle and glass, poured a large brandy.

He rang Superior Chief Calafat and was informed the other was out. He said he'd ring tomorrow. He would probably forget.

As they waited for supper and Juan and Isabel watched the television, Alvarez picked up the bottle of 103 to help himself to another drink.

'Did you hear what the doctor just said, Uncle?' Juan asked.

'No.' Alvarez drank.

'Drinking heavily is like swallowing dynamite.'

He looked at the screen, curious to know why the two children were watching a medical programme rather than cartoons. It was clear the programme, probably encouraged by the government, was aimed at children. The doctor was weedy, his hair was thinning, he had a pinched face with lips thin and straight; just the kind of man to gain satisfaction from denying pleasure to others.

Isabel was in one of her mischievous moods. 'Mummy says you and Daddy drink too much.'

'That is only because she does not understand.'

'What do I not understand?' Dolores demanded, stepping through the bead curtain, a wooden spoon in her right hand.

Alvarez wondered how women always knew when they were being discussed. 'That when it comes to drinking, men and women are different because—'

'Because women exercise self-control.'

'A reasonable amount of alcohol never did anyone any harm.'

'Unless it is a man who decides what is a reasonable amount. Is my husband not back?'

'No, because he's on the booze,' Juan said with glee.

'What did you say?' When Dolores spoke

imperiously, her children cowed.

'I just... I...'

'You will not speak the language of the gutter in this house.'

'But...'

'Well?'

'Nothing.'

'To start a sentence and then admit you have nothing to say is proof of an empty mind.'

'They often talk about boozing on the telly.'

'Much of what is shown on the television is unfit for children; indeed, as much or more should not be watched by any man of decency.' She looked at the table. 'It will be supper in fifteen minutes' time.' There was no missing the unspoken command: Alvarez was not to refill his glass.

He watched her return into the kitchen. She was an admirable woman in so many respects, but she did lack sufficient understanding to know that when a man was exhausted from having worked all hours of the day without a break, a drink was essential.

The sanctimonious doctor on television was still hectoring his viewers and, Alvarez thought scornfully, no doubt would soon list the perils of smoking. If one listened to the medical world, one would eschew everything and die from thirst and starvation.

Eleven

Alvarez drove down to Port Llueso and what had been the first *urbanización* to be built in the north of the island. To the west the mountains formed a backdrop; curling around them was the road which provided a scenically dramatic drive (if one did not suffer from altophobia, as he did) to Hotel Parelona, the luxurious and expensive houses around this, and the even more dramatic drive to the lighthouse on the eastern tip of the island, from which Menorca could occasionally be sighted.

The Langleys lived in a corner bungalow. He rang the front door bell, turned and looked at the garden, which was a blaze of colour. When he'd been young, if flowers were grown at all they would almost invariably be only geraniums and perhaps a rose or two; now the demand was sufficient to call for garden centres where one could buy dozens of different plants, seeds, bulbs, trees, fertilizers, tools, sprays...

'Good morning.'

He started, turned. Langley was leaving middle age; his looks were unremarkable except for a very large mouth. 'Señor Langley?'

'Yes.'

He introduced himself.

'Come on in.'

The small sitting room was adequately, but not luxuriously, furnished. He noted there was no air-conditioning or central heating. Proof that the old myth was nonsense – not every foreigner was a millionaire. Indeed, many British had come to live on the island when prices had been low and their pensions had afforded a very comfortable lifestyle; now prices, following the introduction of the hated Euro, had risen sharply and the state pension provided only a very basic standard of living.

A woman was seated in one of the comfortable but well-worn chairs. 'My wife,' Langley said. 'Inspector Alvarez.'

She smiled a greeting.

She reminded Alvarez of a woman he had once known, not because there was any similarity in appearance, but because she projected an air of emotional warmth. She was not beautiful, would prime no fantasies, but lucky was the man with her.

'Do sit down.'

He sat. 'I apologize for troubling you, Señora, but I have to speak about your car which is, I believe, a yellow Clio.'

'It is,' Langley answered. 'But before we go any further, let me offer you a drink. We were about to pour ourselves one.'

The brandy was just reasonable. Langley offered cigarettes. 'Now, why the interest in our car?' he asked as he sat down.

Once again, Alvarez described the mythical car crash, adding for variety a small dog which had escaped from one car and run away, to the tearful consternation of its owner. Luckily, it had been found the next day. The car which had driven along shortly before the crash had been a yellow Clio and he was asking if this belonged to the Langleys. If it did, perhaps one of them would tell him if they had noticed anything odd about the surface of the road?

'I believe, Inspector, you have met Lavinia?' Langley said, his well-modulated voice still holding a trace of Cornish accent.

'I don't recognize the name.'

'Señora Sewell.'

'Now I know whom you mean.'

'We're very friendly with her and she phoned earlier to tell us about the excitement of a visit from a detective. It was you who spoke to her, I imagine?'

'It was, yes.'

'You were trying to trace a black and white Smart car which had driven along a road just before a bad crash and wanted to identify the owner to ask what the surface of the road was like.'

Alvarez remained silent.

'And now it seems our ancient Clio might also have been on that road at that time. I presume you are trying to trace many cars, so you must be very busy. Then I can lighten your task to some slight degree. Neither

Joan nor I was anywhere near there on the day you mentioned.'

'Then I do not have to bother you further.'

'A short, sharp interview! You'll have another drink?'

Alvarez was uneasy; there was a smile behind the other man's words. 'Thank you, Señor.'

As Langley left with the glasses, his wife initiated a conversation. Had he always lived on the island? What was it like before tourism?

Langley returned, handed one glass to his wife, a second to Alvarez, sat. 'I imagine that even from a very short acquaintance, Inspector, you will have judged Lavinia to be a sharp and intelligent woman?'

'Indeed.'

'She is also what I call instructively inquisitive. So she wondered why so serious a road accident as you described to her had not been reported in her newspaper. After you left, she bought all the Spanish papers she hadn't seen and went through them, searching for such a report. There was none.'

Little old ladies, Alvarez thought, should stick to their tatting.

'It made her wonder if you had reason for hiding the real purpose of your visit. Later, by chance, she met Henry Kerr at the post office and learned you'd visited him and why. Ever more intrigued, she phoned us to ask if we knew what was going on. I laughed and said it was probably nothing. Then you come here and ask us the same questions and I realize she was right to be curious.'

Alvarez reached across to stub out his cigarette in an ashtray. He was a fool to have assumed that despite her obvious doubts, Lavinia had accepted his story.

'Local rumour says you are investigating Jasper Vickers's murder. Is that correct?'

'I am investigating the circumstances of his death.'

'It was an accident?'

'There is no reason to think otherwise.'

'No reason for us to do so or no reason for you to do so?'

Alvarez drank.

'But answer came there none— And this was scarcely odd because he suspected

141

every one.'

'For God's sake, stop it,' Joan said sharply. She spoke to Alvarez. 'My husband has a very warped sense of humour.'

'And curiosity. Because if I'm right—'

'Which you aren't.'

'If I'm right, putting the pieces of the puzzle together in the correct order, the inspector must understand something.'

'You can't talk like that.'

He faced Alvarez. 'Gossip is raised to an art by many ex-pats. We've heard a dozen, or more, different versions of Jasper's death. The most consistent one is that it was not an accident or you, the police, would not be asking so many questions. So who would want to murder Jasper? One opinion must be: anyone who knew him. A more conservative one is the husband or boyfriend of one of the women he's seduced. Though seduction seems the wrong word for enthusiastic co-operation.

'I dismissed all the talk as the usual nonsense beloved of people with nothing to do. But then Lavinia's phone call made me wonder and your visit today confirms it was not nonsense.'

'Gavin, please...' she began.

He interrupted her. 'It has to be asked, if there was no crash and you are uninterested in the surface of any road, why would you present the story to some people? The only answer I can provide is that you are interested in the owners of certain cars. Why should that be of concern to you? Because these cars were known to have been driven frequently to Ca Na Pantella by women on their own, raising the presumption that on each occasion she was about to enjoy Jasper's intimate hospitality? Identify the lady, meet the husband or boyfriend, judge whether he had faced Vickers and inadvertently or deliberately killed him. You have learned that my wife frequently visited Vickers in our Clio—'

'You didn't kill him,' she said violently.

'I know that, but the inspector doesn't.'

She spoke to Alvarez. 'Yes, I often drove up to see Jasper. Gavin always knew I did. And it wasn't for the reason the staff, local ex-pats and you must think...'

'I do not judge when I do not know the

143

facts, Señora.'

'I am a married woman who frequently visited, on my own, a man who was a known libertine and you don't assume I was one of his mistresses?'

'I do not make assumptions.'

She was silent for a moment then said, more calmly than before, 'I don't have to be told I'm not like the glamorous women in his life; I'm glad I'm not. But even so, he did once try to make a pass – reflex action... Are you wondering how I can be stupid enough to imagine you will believe me when Jasper so clearly appeared to have only one reason for being friendly with a woman?'

'Far from it.'

'You're being very diplomatic.'

'It is the truth,' Langley said violently.

'The truth is often more difficult to believe than a lie.' She spoke to Alvarez once more. 'I've always been a keen sailor. My father had a yacht when we lived near Poole and it was he who fired my love of sailing. When old enough, I crewed other people's yachts and sailed in several races, notably the Fastnet.' She was momentarily silent as memory took her back to the past.

'After I married Gavin, I offered to give up sailing, but he was too generous to hear of that. When we came here to live, he bought a thirty-three-foot Swiftsure from a man who was returning to England and I spent hours on the water. Then Gavin had some bad luck—'

'Was a naive fool,' Gavin muttered.

'It is not being naive to help.'

'It is when it ends up in disaster... An old friend, Inspector, got into considerable financial trouble back home and came here to beg me to help him out. He needed more than I'd imagined, but for the sake of the friendship, I lent him what he needed. He never repaid me and around the same time an insurance company in England went bust, taking a nasty amount of our capital with it, so we found ourselves on a greatly reduced income just as the cost of living soared. I had to tell Joan we could no longer afford the running costs of her boat.'

There was a brief silence, which she broke. 'I was down on the quayside, studying a very beautiful yacht, when I noticed one of the halyards was loose. Jasper was aboard and I called out to him and he made it fast, then came ashore and thanked me for telling him. We got talking boats, I mentioned the racing I'd done, he invited me to have a coffee at the Club Nautico. By the time we left there, I had learned or guessed that he knew next to nothing about yachting, that his yacht was purely a status symbol, that he had had a row with his crewman and would like me to help him sail.

'It wasn't difficult to judge the kind of man he was and normally I would have had as little to do with him as possible, but the chance of handling so beautiful a boat ... well, I asked Gavin what he thought.'

'And I,' Langley said, 'told Joan to go ahead despite his reputation. I knew what it would mean to her to be able to sail again and, even if he was a complete rotter, I knew I could trust her implicitly.'

She reached out and briefly put her hand on his. 'So you see, Inspector,' she said, as she withdrew her hand, 'my visits to his place were always connected with his yacht; he needed advice, he wanted me to read about the latest gadget in one of the yachting magazines – he seemed to think that one day something would come along that would make up for his complete lack of seamanship.'

'Thank you for telling me all this, Señora.'

Alvarez left. He sat in his car, but did not immediately drive away. Had he heard the truth or a cleverly concocted story? Often a guilty person would acknowledge there was good reason to suspect him, or her, in the hope that apparent honesty must suggest innocence. Had Joan Langley's reason for a relationship with Vickers merely been to give her the chance to enjoy the fun and pleasure – or so it was claimed – of yachting? Was it likely that Vickers, enjoying the favours of young, beautiful women, would be sexually interested in her? Yet a man's desires could lie beyond logic. And although he believed her to be honest, totally faithful, first impressions could prove very false.

He looked at his watch and was annoyed to note there was still time to continue work and, since he was in the port, he must question Gloria Dudley.

* * *

The front door of the flat opened and he faced a woman, older than she would wish to be thought, auburn hair carefully styled, features which, had they been allowed to be more subtle, would have been very attractive, dressed in a gaily coloured frock which hugged her fashionably slim body.

He introduced himself, explained his reason for calling.

'Surely not now?' she said.

'I fear it has to be now, Señora.'

'Can't you come back tomorrow? Someone's coming here.'

'I will be as brief as possible. It will be more convenient for you than having to come to the station, Señora.'

'Shit! I suppose if you must. But please be quick.'

He followed her through the hall into the large sitting room with its view over the bay. The sun was still relatively high and it bathed the blue water with shafts of sparkling silver. 'You have a wonderful view, Señora.'

'It's all right... I suppose you want to ask about my car?' She sat; her expression was sulky. 'You're asking everyone, aren't you?'

Yet again, he detailed the mythical car crash. Did she own a black Volvo estate?

'Yes, but I haven't been on the road you're talking about in ages. So it couldn't have been my Volvo that was seen.'

'Thank you. Now, I should like to speak to your husband.'

'If I knew where he is, I'd tell you so you could arrest him and chuck him in jail. But I don't. I'm sure he'll be sponging off some-one... If there's nothing more, perhaps you'd leave.'

'I still have some questions.'

'Can't you ask them some other time?'

'I would prefer to do so now.'

'But—' She was interrupted by the door bell. She swore again, hesitated, looked at him. 'I really am sorry, but... Oh, what's the sodding use?' She went into the hall.

He was just able to hear her try, and fail, to convince the visitor to return in half an hour.

Rowena entered the room, came to a stop when she saw him. 'Hullo there.'

He came to his feet, noted the rings on her

marriage finger. 'Good evening, Señora.'

'So who are you?'

He answered her. She had the bumptious manner of the typical English woman who had played hockey, acted in amateur dramatics, and loved horses.

'Fancy finding you here!' She seemed amused. 'I suppose you're asking questions about cars?'

'Among other things.'

'He was just about to go,' Gloria snapped.

'In the circumstances, Señora,' he said, 'I am certain it would be better for both of us if I do return another time.'

He left, took the lift down to the ground floor and went out. Many people were enjoying the late sunshine, sunbathing on the sand, swimming, drinking at the tables set under Tahiti covers. Why had Gloria so clearly not wanted him to meet the woman to whom he had not even been introduced? Because the newcomer was connected with the case? Impossible to know for the moment, so it was a waste of time to theorize. However, throughout his drive back to Llueso, he could not stop doing so.

⋆ ⋆ ⋆

Gloria put the two filled schooners down on the table out on the balcony, sat down.

'I wonder why he came here to ask you about your car?' Rowena asked.

'Who said he did?'

'He did.'

Gloria drank.

'Well?'

'I don't know why he came here.'

'He didn't ask you if it was your car that often went up to Jasper's place?'

'No.'

'Remember telling me you'd never had anything to do with Jasper and that people who said you were seeing a lot of him were liars?'

'No.'

'So was he?'

'Was he what?'

'As good in bed as rumour had him?'

'You've got a dustcart of a mind,' Gloria said furiously.

Twelve

Alvarez marvelled at the apparent ease with which Garau opened the safe in the main bedroom at Ca Na Pantella. The police were fortunate his work was performed legitimately.

'It's all yours,' Garau said as he stepped back. 'Will you want me to relock it when you're finished?'

'I don't think so. I'll take anything of value back to the post and put it in the safe there.'

'Right, then I'll be away.'

The bald, unremarkable-looking man with fingers of magic packed various pieces of equipment into a leather case, left.

Alvarez brought out the contents of the safe and put them on the large bed with barley-sugar-twist corner posts. 2150 euros in hundred- and fifty-euro notes – to one man, spending money, to another a small fortune. There was a stockbrokers' quarterly summary of Vickers's portfolio, a receipt for a year's subscription to the British lottery, several small, attractive pieces of jewellery, each of similar design and in a velvet-lined box – presents for services to be rendered? There were also bank statements from a local bank and two in Liechtenstein, cheque books, a passport, sundry papers including bills and receipts, a couple of letters which, skimmed through, were of no account unless one were Vickers or the two women who had written them, and a double-page spread from a newspaper, on the right-hand side of which was the photograph of an attractive, topless young lady above an article headed 'New forensic techniques will solve major unsolved crimes.' If only it were that easy! He studied the photograph. She was shapely, certainly, but no more so than Pamela Cutler.

He searched the bedroom for something in which to put all the papers, but found nothing suitable. He went downstairs and along to the kitchen where Elena was stirring something in a saucepan on one of the gas rings above the double oven electric stove.

'That smells good,' he said.

'So it should.'

'I need something in which to put the contents of the safe.'

'You still do not think it was an accident?'

'I'm sure it wasn't.'

For a moment, she stirred very vigorously.

'I've come to ask if you can find something in which to put everything to take back to the post. A small suitcase or a holdall would do.'

'Look upstairs in the end room to the right ... Before you go up, perhaps you would like a coffee and a little *coñac*?'

'How did you guess? And perhaps there's a little of the chocolate sponge which by comparison makes ambrosia tasteless?'

'You talk nonsense!' she said, delighted by the praise. 'Sit down and I'll make the coffee.'

He sat. Elena switched on the espresso machine, brought half a chocolate sponge out of a cupboard, put it on the table, set a plate, knife, cup and saucer in front of him.

Temptation had been introduced into the world in order for man to succumb to it. He cut himself a large slice of sponge.

Ana entered the kitchen. 'Come for a meal, have you?' she asked pertly.

'As I have just said to Elena, I have come to dine with the gods.'

'Looking at your plate, you're not leaving them much to eat.'

'You do not speak to the inspector like that,' Elena said.

Ana muttered something, went to sit at the table.

'The inspector needs sugar, milk, *coñac*, and a glass. Perhaps two glasses.'

'I'll make it three.'

'If you're not careful, young lady, you'll be walking.'

'We'll all be doing that as soon as things are sorted out here. And maybe I'll go sooner. A friend has a job in Hotel Presidente and they're looking for another maid. They pay better money than I'll ever get here.'

'And make you earn it.'

'You think I don't work like a galley slave

here?'

'The sugar, milk, glasses and *coñac*,' Elena snapped.

Ana swore, loud enough for Alvarez to regret the crudity of modern youth. She stood, brought a silver sugar bowl out of a cupboard, a bottle of milk from the double refrigerator, and was about to put them on the table when Elena said sharply: 'You pour the milk into a jug.'

'We're entertaining royalty?'

'You're showing that one of us has some manners.'

Bad-temperedly, Ana filled a small jug with milk. She left the kitchen, returned with an unopened bottle of Jaime III.

Having placed the money, jewellery and passport in the post's safe, Alvarez went slowly up to his office, emptied the small holdall and put cheque books, bank statements and papers on the desk. He sat and wondered how long it was going to take to read through and evaluate everything in the hope of finding some reference or financial statement to indicate who had had reason to wish Vickers dead. Or if Vickers had indulged in S & M. He shook his head. Had Vickers been of that persuasion, there would have been an indication of this somewhere in the house, he was sure.

The phone rang. Salas wished to speak to him.

'Good morning, Alvarez.'

He suffered a sense of shock. Salas never offered the courtesy of a greeting...

'How is your investigation into the death of Vickers proceeding?'

'Going along steadily, Señor.'

'Have you uncovered any fresh evidence?'

'The locksmith has finally opened the safe. Those items of no immediate importance, such as money, are in our safe. All the papers, bank statements, and so on are in front of me now and I am going through them.'

'Good. It is heartening to have it confirmed that my inspectors always work to the best of their ability.'

Perhaps Salas thought he was talking to someone else?

'I thought you should know I have re-

ceived a long telephone call from Superior
Chief Calafat in Mahon.'

If Calafat was shouting again, why was
Salas being pleasant?

'On behalf of Inspector Cerda, he has
asked me to convey to you the inspector's
regret at having spoken as he did. By the
same token...'

Alvarez waited. As the silence continued,
he wondered if Salas had finally succumbed
to whatever brain damage he was so obviously suffering from.

'By the same token, I should like to make
the point that if I made any comments that
were erroneous and might have been taken
amiss by you, this was because of the stress
of my great responsibility. I feel certain you
also experience moments when it is difficult
to maintain the necessary level appreciation
of all events.'

He had become certain of nothing, but it
was safer to agree. 'Yes, Señor.'

Salas's voice sharpened. 'You will hold
yourself ready to give Mahon all the assistance you can.'

'But...'

'What?'

'They aren't going to listen to anything I say.'

'They are hardly likely to request assistance in the investigation into the murder of Upton if they are not prepared to accept it.'

'Murder?'

'That is what I said.'

'They insisted it was an accident. Wouldn't listen when I suggested they examined the body more closely, studied the similarity between the nature of the deaths and the many telephone calls between Upton and Vickers. Why do they suddenly agree it might be murder?'

'I understand from Superior Chief Calafat... He was at pains to speak in a most friendly and complimentary manner. I imagine this was an indirect apology for his previous behaviour.' Salas became silent.

'What did you understand from him, Señor?'

'That Evans, described as a friend of Upton's, is so certain Upton was murdered that he went to the Cuerpo and became almost hysterical when they insisted it was an

159

accident.'

'Was he a very close friend?'

'I have no idea.'

'I just wondered if perhaps the two were... That would explain why he seems to have been abnormally upset by Upton's death.'

'You do not credit that a man who enjoys a strong friendship is likely to be upset by the other's death?'

'That is the point I'm making.'

'I am unable to perceive you are making any point.'

'I'm wondering if the two men were partners.'

Salas said, with distaste, 'You are suggesting there was a relationship between them?'

'It's possible.'

'I am sure you could conceive that two marble statues could have a relationship.' He rang off.

Alvarez replaced the receiver. It had been an unusual phone call. In the relatively short time they had been speaking, Salas had swung from being a thoughtful, considerate senior to his normal uncomplimentary, arrogant, rude self.

Thirteen

Alvarez had once suggested to Salas, in provocative jest rather than with any seriousness, that the murderer might be a woman. A woman scorned was to be feared and Vickers must have scorned many. Yet it would have needed physical strength to carry out the murder – and in any case poison was normally a woman's first choice. Yet a woman might be able to answer a question which still puzzled and intrigued him: why had Gloria made it so obvious she did not want him to speak to the newcomer to whom he had not been introduced? Had her manner any bearing on the case?

Mrs Sewell greeted him warmly, upbraided him for not returning before, poured drinks. 'You have come to ask me about another car crash?' she asked mischievously as she sat.

He smiled. 'No, Señora.'

'This is a social call?'

'I have to confess I need to ask you something, but it is a pleasure rather than a duty
to be here.'

'My husband used to say that most com-
pliments were Greek gifts.'

'I spoke the truth.'

She studied him, her brown eyes sharp. 'I
believe you, even though you have lied to
me in the past.'

'Unsuccessfully.'

She chuckled. 'Ask me your question. I
will answer as best I can, and then we will
forget all work and you will tell me about
life on the island before it became a tourist
mecca. I have read that living conditions
were very hard; charcoal burners lived like
hermits up in the mountains, meat was a
luxury denied to townspeople unless they
kept a pig in the mule stable or had friends
or relatives in the countryside. Is all that
true?'

'Yes, Señora, and soon I will tell you all I
know or have heard when young – it is a

pleasure to find a foreigner interested in the history of the island.' He paused, then said: 'Do you know Señora Gloria Dudley?'

'Everyone does. She tends to be rather obvious.'

'Would you think she was a friend of Señor Vickers?'

'So you've come here hoping I will know all the gossip?'

'Of course not, as I said.'

'Certainly you are not an expert liar, Inspector, but this time I'll forgive you because I'm sure you're trying not to hurt my feelings. I am not a gossip, but gossip does seem to favour me. There was talk about her and Jasper, yet if she ever mentioned Jasper, she was always contemptuous about his background, manners, and lifestyle. I have to admit, I thought more than once that this was probably a smokescreen.'

'You think there was a relationship?'

'Probably.'

'Did you ever meet her husband?'

'Malcolm. Often before they parted and he returned to England. I liked him.'

'Why do you think the marriage failed?'

'Because he bored her and she was convinced she could prise enough money out of him to continue living as she thought she was entitled to.'

'Might he have heard rumours about her and Señor Vickers?'

'If he had, he would not have challenged her. In that sense, he was rather a feeble man; not enough backbone to match hers.'

'So he probably would not have spoken to the *señor*?'

'Most unlikely.'

'You seem quite positive?'

'If you'd met Malcolm, you'd know why. Just as you'd accept the impossibility of his murdering Jasper in revenge for Gloria's behaviour.'

He finished his drink. He was no nearer understanding Gloria's behaviour at her flat, but was now prepared to accept that it had nothing to do with Vickers's death.

Seated in his office, Alvarez stared at the telephone for several minutes before he picked up the receiver and dialled Palma.

'Superior Chief Salas's office,' his secretary said with a verbal flourish.

'Inspector Alvarez. I'd like a word with Señor Salas.'

'Wait.'

'Yes?' Salas finally demanded some time later.

'Señor, I should like to report on my investigation into the death of Señor Vickers.'

'For the first time, I understand fully the meaning of the saying "Always expect the unexpected".'

'If you remember...'

'Should you have mentioned the fact to me, I will remember.'

'I have questioned those persons identified by their cars—'

'How is a person identified by his car?'

'Because he or she is the owner.'

'If you know that, how can there be a need for identification?'

'It's the other way round.'

'Upside down, I suggest. Will you never learn how to make an intelligible report?'

'I was going to explain, but you said it was unnecessary.'

'I most certainly said nothing of the sort.'

'When I asked you if you remembered...'

'You expect me to remember what I am not told?'

'No, Señor, unless it was in the past.'

'What was in the past?'

'What you now say you were not told.'

'Alvarez, unless I am to conclude you are speaking in a foreign language, marshal your thoughts and explain in simple words: what is the other way round?'

'The staff...'

'Where?'

'Ca Na Pantella.'

'How can they be the other way round?'

'They aren't.'

'Then in the name of the Tower of Babel, what is?'

'As I have mentioned, the staff described certain cars which frequently visited the house and were driven by women on their own. Since it seemed probable these women were very friendly with Señor Vickers, I set out to identify who they were from their cars since if they were married, their husbands would have had good reason to hate Vickers.'

'You presume that if a married woman visits a man, she is having an affair with him? You cannot comprehend friendship, only the forces of lust? It is impossible to understand – and I have no wish to be enlightened – how anyone could become so perverted in his understanding of human relations.'

'In my experience...'

'You will not sully this conversation by recounting it.'

'I questioned the husbands. In two cases, they were clearly unaware of the extent of their wives' friendship with Vickers, and I learned nothing to indicate they or their husbands had any part in the murder.'

'And the third case?'

'Señor Sewell was well aware of the frequent visits his wife made to Señor Vickers's home and that she frequently went sailing with him when there was no one else aboard the yacht.'

'Have you been able to uncover any evidence against Sewell?'

'No, Señor, because...'

'You lack the initiative to do so?'

'I am convinced Señora Sewell did not have an affair with Señor Vickers.'

'For once, your perverted imagination fails you?'

'On the contrary, I have sufficient imagination to be able to accept what others may find impossible. There are a few women for whom loyalty is more important than life.'

'Without life, there can be no loyalty. Restrict yourself from making absurd and high-flown comments.'

There was a brief silence.

'Sum up your report,' Salas said.

'The facts so far may seem unproductive, Señor, but often the negative can be as positive as the positive. I am now certain that none of those I questioned killed Vickers, which means they can be removed from any list of suspects; much greater attention can be paid to those who remain on it.'

'How many do?'

'For the moment, there is no one.'

'An extraordinary admission! Small wonder that you prefer the negative to the positive.'

'Señor, perhaps for the moment I cannot suggest further suspects since I have no more names of married women who frequently visited Ca Na Pantella on their own. But one must remember that the *señor* was rich – perhaps money provided the motive for his murder—'

'If he was murdered.'

'Since Señor Upton died in similar circumstances in Menorca...'

'You will not repeat your previous assumptions. Have you examined all his personal papers?'

'As I think I mentioned at the beginning, I am doing so.'

'Who benefits under his will?'

'I have been unable to find one. Judging from the kind of man he was, it's very possible he didn't make one.'

'Do his bank statements show regular outgoings sufficient to raise the possibility of blackmail?'

'As yet, I have not found such evidence.'

'Your progress in the investigation is easily summed up. There has been none.'

The line went dead and Alvarez replaced

the receiver. As Felix Sequi had written, "Look not to authority for understanding".

Jaime filled his glass with wine. 'Supper's going to be late,' he said lugubriously.

'Why's that?' Alvarez asked.

'Dolores is seeing Rosa and those two talk and talk and ignore everyone else.'

'She wasn't meeting Rosa,' Juan said as he turned away from the cartoons on television.

'How would you know?'

'She told you she was seeing Eloísa.'

'That's right,' Isabel said loudly.

'Kids think they know everything.' Jaime looked at his watch. 'If she's not back very soon, it'll be too late to do any cooking. These days, they just think of themselves, don't care about anyone else. I come back, exhausted from working hard all day, and she's out enjoying herself.'

'I wouldn't call talking to Eloísa very enjoyable,' Alvarez observed.

'Then why is she doing it?'

Juan answered him. 'Eloísa's ill and

Mother's gone to cook her some supper.'

'That's great to hear! Cook her supper, but not mine.'

'She'll be back soon,' Alvarez said.

'When it suits her, not us. And if we have to eat bread and cheese, that's too bad as far as we're concerned. Years ago, a wife would feel dishonoured to leave her husband to starve.'

'Times change.'

'For the worse for us men.'

They heard the front door. Jaime drank quickly. Dolores came from the *entrada* into the sitting room. Her brightly coloured dress showed she still had a graceful figure; her midnight-dark hair had become ruffled and now partially framed her strongly featured face. 'Is everything all right?'

'I'm hungry,' Juan answered, 'and father says we can only have bread and cheese because you won't do any cooking.'

She came to a halt in front of the bead curtain across the kitchen doorway. 'He has said I am not about to cook a meal? Did he explain why that should be?'

'It's because you don't think of anyone but

yourself.'

'He's talking nonsense,' Jaime said hurriedly.

'You did say that,' Isabel confirmed. 'You came back exhausted from work and you weren't going to have a meal because Mother doesn't care about you, just about herself.'

'I didn't mean it like that.' There was a note of desperation in Jaime's voice.

Dolores, her words encased in ice, said: 'It seems you have already drunk sufficiently liberally to speak words you normally take care to keep hidden.'

'The kids misunderstood what I said.'

'It is your opinion I should never leave the house in order to help someone if this causes you the slightest inconvenience?'

'Of course it isn't.'

'Then why complain when I am away for a few minutes helping Eloísa? And you speak of the exhaustion of work. But it obviously is not so acute as to prevent your helping yourself to many drinks.' She swept through the bead curtain into the kitchen. A moment later, she banged some kitchen utensils together to express her feelings.

The pleasure of having children was questionable, Jaime decided as he drank.

Fourteen

The phone rang.

'You are to fly to Menorca,' Salas said.

'Do what, Señor?'

'My order is too complicated for you to understand?'

'It's just that I don't understand why.'

'The exercise of a little intelligence would provide the answer. The superior chief in Mahon has asked for your help in the investigation into the death of the Englishman, Upton.

'Naturally, I offered to send someone more capable, but he said he would prefer your presence since you had alerted them to the problem of the manner of Upton's death. It is the misfortune of the Menorquin Cuerpo that, not having reached the standard we enjoy, they are content with second best.'

'But how...?'

'You will claim a priority seat on the first civil flight.'

Since Alvarez had never understood why a plane flew, when in the air he always expected it to remember the laws of gravity and crash to the ground; only a couple of brandies were able to contain such fear.

Inspector Cerda was at the airport. A man could hardly be less aptly named; he was lean, chisel-featured, and quick moving. Alvarez had feared that their only telephonic conversation would cause this meeting to be very strained, but Cerda's handshake was firm and his manner friendly.

They left the terminal building and crossed to a Renault saloon in a No Parking area. Cerda settled behind the wheel, started the engine. 'We're seeing Evans at the post in an hour so we've time to have a coffee and a *coñac.*'

It seemed he might be a man after his own heart after all, Alvarez decided.

They drove into Mahon and parked on a solid yellow line in front of a café. They sat at a table in the shadow of a tree from where Alvarez could see much of the famed harbour. It was beautiful, of course, but not to be compared with Llueso Bay.

The waiter took their order and Cerda offered cigarettes. 'I suppose your superior chief told you why we asked you to come over?'

'Only that you'd asked for my assistance, which he judged would be useless.'

'A great recommendation! I've heard your boss is a bit of a bastard.'

Alvarez suffered the strange desire to defend Salas – that he was a complete bastard was not for general dissemination. 'He can be difficult, but most of the time he's no worse than any other senior.'

'Calafat has a tongue like a razor.'

'So I gathered.'

'Sorry about the way things went, but when the doctor said the injuries were wholly consistent with accident and there was no evidence to prove otherwise, I didn't believe...' Cerda held out his hands in a gesture which said the ability to make mistakes was a mortal condition.

'I'd have thought the same and cursed anyone who tried to tell me I didn't know what I was doing.'

'Good of you to say so. Of course, when Evans turned up and shouted murder, I started thinking back to the beginning.'

'How have you made out?'

Cerda remained silent as the waiter came up to the table, put on it two cups of coffee and two glasses of brandy, spiked the bill and hurried away.

They drank. Cerda stubbed out his cigarette. 'I asked the doctor to re-examine the body. Not surprisingly, that made him jump on to his high horse and gallop.' He smiled. 'I'm not the only one to resent the suggestion I may have missed something! Anyway, he eventually did as asked. There were no cuts under the chin, no suggestion of masking tape having been used, and nothing to challenge the original verdict of accident.

'I returned to Upton's house and, with a colleague, searched it from top to bottom. In the floor of the kitchen, we found a small space under a loose tile. In this were several hundred euros in notes, along with a pass-port and bank statements. These last show-ed that Upton had received similar sums regularly and these have been identified as having come from a bank in Llueso. Black-mail? Or was it just coincidence the pay-ments had come from Llueso? Most pressing of all, who else had a motive for murder? If no one, then we are back with accident and the obvious answer, that he was so drunk he tripped and fell down the winding stairs – very easily done, I'd add, since they are crude and turn a half circle – and bashed his head on a stone corner.

'But then we have Evans crying murder. The relationship between him and Upton will have left him emotionally shattered and unwilling to accept he's lost his companion through sheer drunken stupidity, but he has raised several potentially interesting facts. But how factual are they? Many questions to which I'm hoping you'll provide the answers.'

'Don't hope too hard. I was convinced there was a connexion between the deaths of Vickers and Upton – in other words, murder – but have failed to find the proof. Equally, I have failed to identify Vickers's murderer since all the suspects who there was reasonable reason to believe had a motive for his death are almost certainly innocent. To tell the truth, I'm here hoping to learn something from you to help my investigation.'

Cerda laughed. 'The blind looking for a lead from the blind!' He checked the time. 'There's time for another coffee and *coñac*.'

The interview room had walls painted a depressing brown, the ceiling a flaky white, the bars across the single small window, black. The wooden table, showing the wear of many years, was set against one wall and on it was a tape recorder. The four wooden chairs might have been discarded from somewhere.

Evans, helped by a nudge in the back, entered.

'This is Inspector Alvarez from Llueso in Mallorca. He's here to help us,' Cerda said.

Evans looked at Alvarez, then hurriedly away.

'Sit down.'

Evans sat. He was tallish, good-looking, well built, and moved with muscular ease; his obvious nervousness indicated a lack of self-confidence.

'I'd like you to tell us all you can about your friendship with Señor Upton...' Cerda began.

'He was murdered by that bastard. But you won't believe me. Doesn't matter how often I tell you.' Evans's Spanish was fluent and only the occasional word was mispronounced.

'It's not that we disbelieve you. But we have to make certain of the facts before we can accept what you say. That's just the way we work.'

'Johnny said he'd be done for. I thought he was just angry, saying wild things, like he did. Only it wasn't, was it?' He rubbed his eyes, fiddled with his T-shirt. 'We was going on a cruise. Johnny wanted to see Knossos. Kept talking about it and showing me photos and saying what we'd do when

we was there; he'd bought a new digital
camera. And then that man came. And
killed Johnny. And there won't be no trip to
Knossos.'

'I'm sorry.'

Trite words, but they seemed to help
Evans overcome a surge of grief.

'When did you first meet Señor Upton?'

'What's that matter?'

'Help us do things our way. That will give
us the best chance of finding out the truth.'

He spoke in a more controlled manner. 'I
was here on holiday and we were in a bar
and got talking. Later, I said I must get back
to my job at home, but Johnny said to stay
because he'd enough money for the both of
us.'

'He was wealthy?'

'He had plenty.'

'Where did it come from?'

'I asked him once.'

'What was his response?'

'Came from an inheritance. So I asked,
from his father? That made him so mad he
lost his temper and threatened to chuck me
out.'

'Why did it so annoy him?'

'How could I know?'

'Was he a violent man?'

'Not to me, he wasn't, but he had a terrible quick temper. Even something small would have him shouting.'

'What kind of something.'

'There was the phone calls for a start.'

'Which ones?'

'From Mallorca.'

Cerda looked at Alvarez, indicated he should take up the questioning.

'From whereabouts in Mallorca?' Alvarez asked.

'Wouldn't know,' Evans answered.

'You've no idea where they were from?'

'No.'

'Or what they were about?'

'They sent him shouting mad. That's all I know.'

'Was he receiving these calls when you first knew him?'

'I don't think so.'

'So when do you reckon they started?'

'Maybe the beginning of the year.'

'He never said anything about them afterwards?'

'Just cursed and swore.'

'Did he phone Mallorca very often?'

'Can't say. He'd go into another room and shut the door so as I couldn't hear.'

'What do you suppose he didn't want you to hear?'

'Look, him and me were together, but sometimes he kind of lived his own life.'

'Did he know many people here?'

'No.'

'Why was that?'

'Like he said, most of 'em weren't our kind.'

'So few people came to the house?'

'Mostly just them that played poker. Johnny loved his poker.' He stared into space. When he next spoke, his voice was distant. 'Used to go on at me because I was no good; said I got too excited when I had a good hand, so everyone knew and threw in.'

'From what you mentioned earlier, someone came here whom you hadn't met before and wanted to speak to your friend?'

'I let the murdering bastard in. I let him in.' Distress distorted his voice.

'What makes you so certain this stranger killed your friend?'

'Because when Johnny saw him, he was ... he was angry, but also frightened and I never seen that before. When they went into the other room, I heard 'em shouting like there was going to be real trouble.'

'What was the row about?'

'Can't say.'

'Let's get something clear. Is it because of this row that you claim the other man was the murderer?'

'After he'd gone, Johnny was in a terrible state, cursing, saying if he didn't do something quick, he was done for. And if ever I told anyone about who had come to the house, he'd wrap my guts around my neck.'

'Did you ask what the trouble was?'

'I'm not a bleeding fool. If he'd completely lost his rag, he'd have worked me over before he knew what he was doing.'

'Will you please describe the man whom you think murdered Señor Upton.'

'I ain't no good at that sort of thing.'

'We'll take it little by little. Was he English?'

'Yeah.'

'Tall, short, thin or fat?'

'Just ordinary.'

'Did he speak with a regional accent?'

'Spoke smart. Only it weren't right,' he added.

'How do you mean?'

'There's them that talk smart naturally and them that has to try.'

'What sort of age was he?'

'Maybe forty.'

'Handsome?'

'Real sharp.'

'Would you think he was an old friend of Señor Upton?'

'Johnny knew him all right, but he wasn't no friend.'

'After he'd gone, did you learn why he'd called?'

'I said already, Johnny wasn't talking and didn't like me asking.'

'Did he ever mention Mallorca?'

'No.'

'Never talked about someone he knew who lived there?'

'No.'

Alvarez turned to Cerda and nodded, to indicate he had no more questions to ask.

Cerda spoke to Evans. 'Thank you for coming here.'

'You won't listen. I keep telling you, that bastard killed Johnny. But you won't believe me, will you?'

'When we identify him, we'll question him and learn if you're correct.'

Evans stood, his expression one of bitterness and sorrow. He turned, hurried out of the interview room.

Cerda offered cigarettes. 'I may be wrong, Enrique, but I think you can make a very good stab at identifying the mysterious caller.'

'It's a jump in the dark since Evans's description could fit half the male population,' Alvarez answered, 'but the circumstances being what they are...'

'You're nominating Vickers?'

'I'll ask them back home to fax a copy of his passport photo and we can show that to Evans.'

'Let's assume you're right. What was the nature of the relationship and why did

Vickers drive Upton into a rage?'

'I've no idea.'

'That always makes for a good start! Suppose you make the call from my office and then we have lunch at a small restaurant in the countryside where they greet you with a glass of *hierbas* and cook a leg of lamb over charcoal?'

On Monday, Evans again reluctantly entered the interview room.

'Thanks for coming along,' Cerda said.

He sat, moved uneasily on the chair. 'I told you all I know, honest to God.'

'We've no reason to doubt that.'

'Then why d'you want me back here?'

'Inspector Alvarez will show you something.'

Alvarez brought an unused envelope from his pocket and out of this drew the faxed photograph of Vickers. 'Do you recognize this man?' he asked, holding it out.

Evans hesitated, as if fearful of touching it, but finally took it. He stared at the photo, shouted: 'That's him!'

'Who?'

'Him what came to the house.'

'Are you certain?'

'You think I can't recognize the murdering bastard? When are you going to arrest him? You ain't told me who he is.'

'And are not going to,' Cerda said quietly, 'until we have proof.'

'Ain't I given you all the proof you need?'

'I'm afraid not.'

'You can't be bothered to do nothing, can you, because it's the likes of me?'

'What you have told us is not proof that this man murdered your friend,' Alvarez said. 'So we have to go and find that missing proof. It would make no difference if you were a duke or a dustman, we work the same.'

'I ... me and Johnny ... we was going to stay together.'

'It has been a tragedy for you. One has to hope that time will lessen it.' Ridiculous words. Had time lessened the tragedy of Juana-Maria's death for him?

'I want to go,' Evans said.

'Then go.'

He stood, held on to the back of the chair

as if for support, stumbled out.

Alvarez reached across the table for the photograph.

'If it was murder, the motive must come from the past, surely?' Cerda said.

'It would seem so.'

'Was Upton ever in Mallorca?'

'That is something I'll have to check. I'll need a photo of him – would you organize that for me?'

'Of course. You know, Enrique, until we uncover a motive, I don't think we are going to move forward.'

'More likely backwards.'

'A pessimist after my own heart.'

Fifteen

Alvarez dialled and when the connection was made, identified himself.

'Wait,' ordered the plum-voiced secretary.

She must have been head girl of her class and then head girl of the school, he thought. No doubt she was still remembered by teachers as a perfect pupil and by her contemporaries as obnoxious.

'What is it?' Salas demanded.

'Inspector Alvarez, Señor. Since I am back home—'

'Illness is to be reported to Personnel, not to me.'

'I am not ill.'

'Then do you know what the time is?'

'Yes, of course.'

'Why are you at home when it's halfway

through the morning?'

'I am not at home, Señor.'

'Then why the devil say you are?'

'When I said I was *back* home, I did not mean I was *at* home.'

'Even a psychiatrist would have difficulty in understanding your inability to talk sense.'

'I was trying to explain I was back here after having been away from the island. As you ordered, I flew to Menorca and met Inspector Cerda. He admitted he could not be certain about the details of Upton's death, despite Evans's evidence, and was hoping I would be able to help him.'

'A man of small expectation.'

'It was established that while Vickers's connexion with Upton was obvious, there was no evidence that other once-possible suspects had any interest in Upton.'

'Why do you say "once-possible" suspects?'

'Because when I began questioning them, that was what they became.'

'Are you now saying, in typical convoluted manner, that you no longer consider any of them to be a suspect?'

'In a way.'

'So you have spent endless time conducting an investigation without the slightest result.'

'I don't think it's fair to put it like that.'

'Then perhaps you will tell me how you would describe your failure?'

'I have been able to eliminate many names. As you have so often pointed out, negative evidence can be as important as positive evidence.'

'It is you who constantly maintains that thesis. Out of necessity, of course, since you are much more conversant with the negative than the positive. Do you have other suspects to question?'

'As I think I have said, Señor, I regret not.'

'Have you ascertained a motive for Vickers's death?'

'Not yet.'

'Was Upton murdered, as you have insisted, or was his death due to a drunken accident, as the evidence and medical findings hold?'

'It is still difficult to be certain, despite

Evans's evidence.'

'You insisted Vickers's death was murder, not accident, largely on the evidence of Upton's murder; if the nature of Upton's death cannot be accurately named murder, then neither can Vickers's.'

'It is not that simple.'

'Naturally, with you in charge of the investigation.'

'As I suspected, Evans was Upton's boy-friend...'

'You find it necessary to introduce the fact?'

'It is important since it explains why he's in a position to offer evidence of what happened. Evans has identified Vickers as the man who visited Upton and had a bitter row with him. Upton had said that Vickers would do for him – obviously a very strong indication he believed his life was threatened by Vickers. Inspector Cerda has uncovered evidence which may point to blackmail and it's possible confirmation of this will be found in Vickers's bank statements...'

'You have not searched for and found such evidence?'

'Not yet.'

'You have not finished checking the statements or have failed to grasp the significance of what you have seen? You raise your inefficiency to fresh heights.'

'Even if figures make it reasonably certain Vickers was being blackmailed, that is not going to help solve the nature of Upton's death and, assuming he was murdered, the identity of his murderer.'

'There can be no doubt Vickers was the man who visited Upton?'

'None.'

'It has not occurred to you that since Vickers died before Upton, Upton may have murdered *him* – if indeed Vickers was murdered?'

'I have considered the possibility, Señor, but I don't think it's very likely. Why kill the goose?'

'What the devil has a goose to do with anything?'

'The one which lays the golden egg, Señor. Why would Upton kill the man he was blackmailing?'

'Did Upton visit Ca Na Pantella?'

'I don't yet know.'

'Because you cannot be bothered to find out.'

'I cannot do anything until I receive a photo of Upton from Menorca.'

'You've thought to ask for one?'

'Of course.'

'You have more faith in your competence than I. When you receive the photo, you will immediately question the staff and discover whether Upton ever visited there. Is that quite clear?'

'Yes, Señor.'

The line went dead.

Alvarez stared at the faxed photo of Upton on his desk. Not a man he would trust. A decision he could not justify, or even explain.

He had been ordered to take the photo to Ca Na Pantella as soon as he received it and question the staff, but it was already six and it was reasonable to suppose that one or more of them had left the house. Much more practical to wait until the morning.

★ ★ ★

Ana opened the front door. 'You again! You're out of luck this time.'

He stepped into the hall. 'There's no one but you here?'

'They're all here, but she's not baked a sponge.'

'That is more than bad luck, it is a catastrophe.'

'She says there's no point in cooking one when no one eats it.'

'I've seen her tucking in with real enthusiasm.'

'Of course you have, but she's decided it's started giving her indigestion. That's only because she eats so much of it.'

'It's selfish to think only of herself and not of you and Diaz.'

'I'm on a diet and he has never had any.'

'I can't think why.'

'He doesn't like chocolate.'

'I meant, why you are on a diet.'

'Why d'you think? I don't want to bulge.'

A little bulging would be to her advantage.

'What do you want this time?'

'To show each of you a photograph.'

'Why?'

'You'll find out.'

In the kitchen, Elena was cooking *sopas Mallorquinas*. She greeted Alvarez, offered him coffee, a brandy, and some biscuits of a kind that the *señor* had so liked.

It was the first time he had eaten shortbread. His disappointment at the lack of chocolate sponge diminished. As Ana refilled his glass and cup, he brought out the photograph of Upton and showed it to her.

'Have you ever seen this man?'

After a moment she said, 'No. And I don't reckon I want to.'

It was interesting that her judgment matched his. 'He's never visited the house?'

'Not as far as I know.'

He passed the photograph to Elena. She held it at a distance, then brought it closer to her eyes. Eventually she crossed to a working surface on which was her handbag and brought out a pair of spectacles. 'He's never been here,' she said.

One more dead end. He drank some brandy.

'Who is he?' Ana asked.

'Someone who knew Señor Vickers.'

197

'What's it matter if he came here?'

He didn't answer.

'You think it was him?'

'Do I think it was who?'

'The man who killed the *señor*.'

'No. But he died himself, very soon after the *señor*.'

'So he was something—'

'Give over,' Elena snapped. 'It's the inspector asks questions, not you.'

'He's not complaining.'

'Because he's too well mannered to tell you to shut up.'

Ana spoke to Alvarez. 'Does it annoy you?'

It didn't, but it would be stupid not to agree with Elena since she might soon decide that it was not the chocolate sponge that gave her indigestion. 'Just a little.' He ate the last piece of shortbread, finished the coffee into which he had poured some of the brandy. 'D'you know where I'll find Diaz?'

'Watering the vegetables,' Ana answered. 'Leastwise, that's where he was just before you arrived.'

He thanked Elena for his second *merienda* of the day, then left the kitchen. The vegetable garden, beyond the lantana hedge at the end of the lawn, was farmed by Diaz in traditional style; mattock-drawn irrigation channels and plants grown on the raised soil between these. Water from a *cisterna* was fed into the first channel; when this was full, it was plugged with the earth from opening the second channel, and so on.

Diaz, mattock at the ready, stood at the head of a channel along which grew aubergines, many beginning to colour.

'It's a long time since I saw aubergines as good as those,' Alvarez said in Mallorquin.

Diaz was silent.

'And the peppers next door look as good as any you'll find.'

'It's strange.' Diaz opened one channel and blocked the previous one.

'What is?'

'How so many people start telling me how wonderful everything looks when it's ready for picking.'

'My praise is genuine. I'm not asking for anything.'

'Then you won't be disappointed when you get nothing.'

'What do you intend to do with all the vegetables when there's no *señor* here to eat them?'

'What business is that of yours?'

'None.'

Diaz hawked and spat.

Many would have been annoyed at his open contempt for authority, but Alvarez was not. The sense of arrogant independence and equality had supported Mallorquins through invasions, occupations and persecutions, given them a pride in themselves.

'Have a look at this.' He brought the photograph out of his pocket.

Diaz took it, turned away from the direct sunlight.

'Have you ever seen him?'

'No.'

Alvarez took the photograph back. Diaz opened another channel, closed the previous one.

'Do you have a problem with water in high summer?' Alvarez asked.

'There's two wells and one of 'em never dries.'

'Makes growing a lot easier.'

'How would you know?'

'I was born on a farm and worked in the fields.'

'It was a long time ago, from the size of your belly.'

'If I had money, I'd go back to farming.'

'If men had tails, they'd swing from the trees.'

One more channel opened, one more blocked.

'Did the *señor* ever do any gardening?'

'Him? Didn't believe in doing something himself when he paid someone else to do it. In any case, he'd be scared of hurting himself. When he was cutting roses for the house – some big party – he pricked himself on a thorn and you'd have thought he was going to bleed to death.'

'You told me before he was very nervous.'

Diaz had reached the last channel. He crossed to the *cisterno*, into which water was pumped from one of the wells, and closed the outlet valve.

Alvarez looked across the land. 'One knows what heaven's like when one lives here.'

'Unless one has to work in high summer when the mountains bottle up the heat and it's like being in a furnace. But what would you know about that? Your job seems to be to stand around and talk bloody daft.'

Alvarez toyed with the idea of proving he was just as capable as Diaz at working the land but it was a very hot day and un-accustomed labour could prove fatal.

Sixteen

Alvarez ate a mouthful of *lubina con piñones y passas*, careless of the pleasure the subtle flavours provided. Salas had, for once, been correct. Considered on their own, the circumstances of Vickers's death had not established murder. The cuts under his neck might have been caused by something other than a knife being held against the skin – difficult to think what, but experience showed the most unlikely things often happened. The missing hairs on the wrists could have been removed by something other than masking tape. The bruised mouth and lips, the loosened tooth, could have been the result of a drunken fall. Yet from the beginning, he had instinctively known this was murder. A judgment Salas would refuse to acknowledge because he was a man of few received impressions.

Then had come news of Upton's death. A criminal who carried out one crime successfully would almost always repeat the method when carrying out a second, believing himself clever enough to fool authority again and again. So when one knew Vickers had been in frequent telephonic communication with Upton, what could be more logical than to connect the two deaths? Evans's claims had seemed to confirm Upton's death as murder. Vickers's death had been named murder... All logical until Evans's evidence proved to be unreliable. Which in turn led to the conclusion that Upton's death might have no connexion with Vickers's and so destroyed the certainty that Vickers had been murdered and not died in a drunken accident.

With rare exceptions, motive was one of the best clues to identifying a murderer. He had initially identified only the one motive for Vickers's murder: the revenge of a cuckolded husband. Yet he had questioned the husbands of those wives whom he had suspected had been unfaithful and there was no good reason to suspect any of them. Was there a possible motive that had nothing at all to do with wives and furious husbands? Cerda claimed to have uncovered evidence of blackmail – a possibility he had yet to check – but how could that prove a motive for Vickers's murder when he was the one being blackmailed? Lacking any further motive, and accepting logic, it seemed that perhaps Vickers's death had, after all, been accidental. So the whole investigation might have been useless...

'You are not eating. You find the meal inedible?' Dolores asked with the sweetness of quinine.

He jerked his mind back to the present. 'The tuna is superb.'

'It is sea bass.'

'I have been fooled by the miracle of the sauce of garlic, peppers, and...'

'The sauce is made from onions, pine nuts, raisins, rosemary, white wine, and butter. It takes endless time to make successfully – which clearly I have failed to do – in the furnace of a kitchen because my husband will not mend the fan. Foolishly, as I sweated and my arms ached, I consoled myself with the thought that my suffering would be rewarded by the pleasure with which the meal would be eaten. You persuade me I should have saved myself the pain and served a simple and quickly made dish, such as *gabanzas*.'

Alvarez hastened to rectify his error. 'I was thinking.'

'Not about what you were eating.'

There was only one way of assuaging her antagonism and avoiding her threat of a meal of *gabanzas*. 'I was worrying about the trouble I'm in.'

'Trouble? How serious?'

As hoped, her anger was instantly gone and replaced by compassion; let any member of the family be in trouble and she knew only the need to help. 'The superior chief is shouting because he reckons I've made a complete mess of my investigation.'

'Madrileños believe that no one but themselves is capable of anything.'

'I suppose Salas has some justification.'

'A man like him needs none.'

'Salas wanted the case sorted out very quickly, but it's still unsorted. I've worked as hard as possible, without result. Rather, the result has proved muddled and incorrect. It's easy to guess what he'll write about me in his annual review that gets sent to Madrid.'

'Tries hard, but never succeeds,' Jaime suggested.

Dolores turned to face her husband. 'Had I not known you were born in Llueso, I would be certain it was in Madrid.'

'Why d'you say that?'

She turned back to Alvarez once more. 'So what will the pompous little man say about you to his superior in Madrid?'

'That I have conducted myself with my usual ability and enjoyed the usual result: failure.'

'Isn't that what I suggested?' Jaime asked.

She ignored her husband. 'Then you must complain, Enrique.'

'Wouldn't do any good.'

Her compassion was beginning to fray. 'So you will do nothing? You will let him un-justly slander you? Are you a man or a mouse? If he is so stupidly unfair, don't sit there and squeak, write and complain.'

'You don't understand.'

'Can any woman understand a man's weak stupidity?'

'An official complaint has to pass through the superior chief's hands. He'd either bury mine or make very certain I regretted ever making it.'

'It is easy for a mouse to find reason to retire.'

'Especially when there's a trap ahead,' Jaime sniggered.

'My dear mother was right when she said the heaviest burden a wife has to bear is her husband. Have you both finished eating?'

'I have,' Alvarez said. 'But I'm wondering if there could possibly be a little more?'

'There is no need to force yourself unwillingly to eat in the mistaken belief that will please me.'

'It's to please myself.'

'What man ever considers anyone else?'

Alvarez stared at the mass of papers, cheque books and cheque stubs, which were spread out on his desk. It must take hour upon hour to check through everything, correlate figures, ascertain – when he received figures from Mahon – whether Upton had been receiving regular sums which could be matched with payments made by Vickers. And what was to be gained from such a Herculean effort? If there had been blackmail, what would there be to identify the subject of it? How could it have a bearing on either's death when no blackmailer was going to murder his victim and thereby bring an end to profit? All his past work had been useless, his future work seemingly no less so... Unless, that was, he postulated that Vickers had ensured he was in a position to face Upton's publication of the criminal or disgraceful episode in question, bringing the blackmailing to a sudden halt and placing Upton in danger of arrest. And then Upton, who, in order to save himself from the charge of blackmail, had to murder Vickers...

This was ridiculous. The evidence could not warrant such a possibility. He was confusing himself into chaos. To save himself

from further lunacy, he would go to Club
Llueso for his *merienda*, even if it was rather
early.

He had just reached the doorway when the
phone rang. He ignored it. If the call was of
any importance, the caller would phone
again.

She did, at a quarter to twelve, soon after
Alvarez had returned from a *merienda*
prolonged by meeting an old friend.

'This is the third time I have tried to speak
to you,' said Salas's secretary in her most
plumy voice.

'I had to leave the post.'

'And did not carry your mobile?'

'It refuses to work.'

'Perhaps if you switched it on, it would
agree to do so. The superior chief has asked
me to inform you that Inspector Pocavi will
arrive this afternoon.'

'Arrive where?'

'In Llueso, of course.'

'Why?'

'You have not read your instructions?'

'I haven't received any to read.'

'Wait.'

He stared gloomily through the unshuttered window. Pocavi must have a case that had some connexion with Llueso. By reputation, he was a man who would ask for assistance without a thought to the extra work this would cause others. There were those who said he was heading for high rank. Such men were to be avoided.

'Alvarez.'

'Yes, Señor.'

'Do I understand you claim not to have received my orders?'

'No, Señor, and yes.'

'Would you care to add a perhaps and a maybe?'

'No, I have not received them; yes, you are correct that is what I said to your secretary.'

'Why have you not received them?'

'I have no idea.'

'I find it extraordinary that the mail to Llueso is so much more unreliable than to anywhere else on the island.'

'Perhaps it is because we are furthest away from Palma.'

'Kindly don't talk nonsense. My orders

were to inform you that Inspector Pocavi will be joining you this afternoon.'

'Why?'

'To take charge of the investigation into Señor Vickers's death.'

'How do you mean, to take charge?'

'You are incapable of appreciating even the simplest direction? You will work under his command.'

'But he holds the same rank as me.'

'Which, no doubt, he finds irrational.'

'I'll be working *with* him, not under his command.'

'You may choose your own semantics.'

'Why is he taking any part in my investigation?'

'Because he is a very competent officer with an unmatched knowledge of how successfully to conduct a case. With him in command, there will be no lottery of accident or murder, no fear of using one mistaken judgment to validate another. You will give Inspector Pocavi all possible assistance and refrain from any initiative of your own. Is that clear?'

'Señor, I insist—'

'Inspectors do not insist when speaking to their superior chief.' Salas rang off.

Alvarez replaced the receiver. To be called upon to obey the orders of a fellow inspector was a humiliation not to be borne. He would resign and give as his reason Salas's intemperate leadership which had led him to demote one of his inspectors without the slightest justification; he lacked any ability to appreciate a man's work and so unthinkingly trampled on his pride... But senior officers always believed their fellow colleagues and never their juniors. Salas would call him unreliable, incompetent, less than an asset to the Cuerpo. Rather than resigning, he might well be dismissed for incompetence and insulting his superior chief, which would mean he would lose his pension... Yet if it was a matter of principle, which it was, should it matter what the consequences were? Faced with an insoluble problem, he leant over, opened the bottom right-hand drawer of the desk, and brought out the bottle of Soberano and a glass.

Seventeen

Alvarez climbed the stairs, paused to regain his breath, entered his office. Pocavi, who had been seated at the desk, came to his feet. 'Good to meet you, Enrique.' He came round and held out his hand.

Much too moist, which was always a bad sign, Alvarez thought as he shook hands. And what made the other think they were on first-name terms?

'I'm glad you've finally arrived. I was becoming worried you might be ill and not here to assist me.'

A typically roundabout way of saying that he was a little late.

'I hope you don't mind my commandeering your desk, but I must have something to work on. Naturally, I have told one of the

cabos to find you another desk. In the mean-
time, draw up a chair and we can discuss the
cases.'

Alvarez resented the over-friendly manner, certain it was merely a hypocritical
assertion of authority. He disliked Pocavi's
styled hair, smoothly shaven face no doubt
patted with some poncy aftershave lotion,
thin lips incapable of an honest smile, neatly
knotted tie, city suit, handkerchief in the top
pocket of the coat, and the final affectation
of dark glasses.

He moved a chair away from the wall and
sat.

'Let me say at the very beginning, Enrique, that I hope you bear no resentment at
my taking command of the investigation
since officially we are of the same rank.'

Pocavi had placed emphasis on 'officially',
not considering their ranks to be equal in
standing.

'When he briefed me, which he did at
some length, Superior Chief Salas indicated
there had been some confusion over the
nature of the deaths of Señor Vickers and
Señor Upton. Indeed, he went so far as to

say...' He stopped.

'Say what?'

'He has a great sense of humour, would you not agree?'

'I can't say I've ever noticed that.'

'Perhaps that is a side of him that he does not unveil to everyone. When he mentioned the confusion, he compared the course of your investigation to blowing away the seedling heads of a dandelion. Very amusing, don't you think?'

He did not.

'You'll appreciate the simile. When young, we blow the seeds to find out whether she loves me or loves me not and when the last seed flies, that is the answer.'

'When I was young, I worked on the land all hours it was light and there was no time for girls.'

'Of course, life was very much rougher then.'

For most, but not for the few such as Pocavi's family. They would have eaten meat regularly, drunk Marqués de Riscal, or even Vega Sicilia, and regarded peasants with amused contempt.

'The superior chief is of the opinion that you are wrong to consider both deaths as murders before they can be proved to be so beyond doubt. However, being far too open-minded to consider himself omniscient, he has, in consideration of you, asked me to end the confusion which has so delayed your ability to reach a conclusion.'

'There isn't any confusion.'

'I hesitate to mention this, but don't you think there must have been a considerable amount since your judgments have suffered so many volte-faces?'

'The trouble has been the way in which the evidence has appeared.'

'In bits and pieces which didn't fit?' Pocavi smiled a mean smile. 'Suppose we make a start by your detailing the course of your investigation. Incidentally, it might be best to raise a small point now, before you start. The superior chief mentioned that you were addicted to assumptions and unwilling to accept they can be open to great error. I think it will be best if, from now on, we eschew all assumptions.'

There was a knock on the door and two

cabos, carrying a heavy, well-worn wooden desk, slowly and carefully entered the room.

'Where do you want it?' asked the younger man, slightly breathlessly.

'Put it there.' Pocavi pointed.

No longer allowed to decide where he wanted something put in his office, Alvarez thought bitterly. But then, of course, it was no longer his office.

They put the desk down with a thump. 'Weighs a tonne,' said the elder man as he massaged his back.

'Thirsty weather,' said the younger, staring at the right-hand side of the desk at which Pocavi sat.

Alvarez was alarmed. It seemed possible the *cabo* knew he kept a bottle of brandy in the bottom drawer, a fact he had always taken great care to conceal.

But, since there was no response to the observation, the *cabos* left.

'You can begin your report,' Pocavi said.

Alvarez spoke at length.

'Has the doctor who examined Vickers's body not offered his judgment as to the cause of the wounds on the neck?'

'Typically, he only said what might be possible.'

'Why do you say typically?'

'Doctors, in particular Doctor Llabres, don't like to be definite for fear of being proved wrong.'

'One could say that that also applies to some in our profession. I presume you have not seriously considered further the possibility of death occurring in the course of an S and M session?'

'Not since there was no evidence to support this anywhere in the house.'

'I understand from what you've been saying that you have also dismissed the possibility of the cuts having been caused while shaving?'

'Yes, because—'

'I know what you are going to say.'

Then there was no point in saying it.

'I have discovered over the years, thanks to a reasonable degree of success, that it always pays to think laterally. Would you agree?'

'Probably.' If he knew what that meant.

'A man normally shaves his neck downward so it seems unlikely those horizontal cuts could have been so caused. But if one investigates the growth of hairs on one's neck, what does one find?'

'They get longer.'

'Most amusing. After I learned of the problem of the cuts on the neck, I studied the hairs on my own neck after a day's growth and before shaving. I was surprised, even disconcerted, when on very close examination it became clear a few hairs had escaped several shaves and were quite long – I emphasize that they were not readily visible since they were single and solitary. It might have appeared they were the result of sloppy shaving had I not always shaved with my usual skill and concentration. An even closer look at my neck revealed these hairs grew at a different angle from the majority and could be, and were, missed by a downward stroke of a razor. If Vickers paid great attention to his appearance, which one must expect him to have done in view of his lifestyle, he might well have shaved sideways after shaving downwards; then, due to the angle of the razor blade, it could have nicked the flesh.'

'It sounds very complicated and conjectural and, if you will forgive me saying so, rather far-fetched.'

'Only to someone who lacks the ability to consider facts clearly.'

'But perhaps you are unique in more ways than one and no one else grows hairs as you do. Aren't you assuming rather a lot, contrary to the superior chief's wishes?'

'You are, of course, failing to distinguish an assumption based on known facts and one based on presumptions which are doubtful when not fallacious. What I have been trying to explain is why the direction of the cuts does not necessarily prove that they could not have been caused during shaving.'

'I don't agree.'

'Explain why not.'

'The *señor* used an electric razor.'

There was a silence, finally broken by Pocavi. 'It did not occur to you to mention that fact initially?'

'You said you knew what I was going to say so there seemed no point in repeating the information.'

221

Pocavi began to drum on the desk with his fingers. 'When I came here, I hoped we were going to be able to work together to the benefit of both us and the case.' He stopped drumming. 'We will move on to the hairs on the wrists. The line where they were missing was distinct?'

'Very.'

'In the same position on each arm?'

'Within millimetres.'

'Was there any residue on the skin to indicate something similar to masking tape had been used to tie them together?'

'No.'

'The doctor agrees they were tied together?'

'He accepts they might have been.'

'So once again, you have no proof to support your assumption?'

'Perhaps one of us should tie his wrists together with masking tape and examine the result, very closely, when the tape is ripped off?'

'Perhaps you would care to do that?'

He would not. It might be quite painful.

'The superior chief said you were checking the accounts of Vickers to determine whether he had been subjected to blackmail by Upton. What conclusion have you reached?'

'None, so far.'

'Why is that?'

'I haven't had time to complete the task.'

'The superior chief did mention that you seldom had the time to do the work that needed doing. We'll examine the figures now.'

Alvarez looked at his watch.

'You are meeting someone?'

'I was wondering if it was time for *la merienda*.'

'When on duty, it is never time for that. And perhaps I should also mention that for lunch, we will eat sandwiches. I notice they are sold at the local filling station and they looked reasonably fresh so there is no problem in obtaining them.'

'I always eat at home.'

'The change will be very beneficial to your work.'

'My sister's cooking a very special meal today.'

'A celebration?'

'It's her husband's birthday.'

'Then perhaps there should be an exception. But from tomorrow onwards, lunch for both of us will be sandwiches.'

'You are going to do what?' Dolores said disbelievingly.

Alvarez repeated what he'd said.

'Is his wife so poor a cook he is reduced to living like a tramp?'

'Maybe he's scared she'll add strychnine.' He refilled his glass. 'He's a workaholic.'

'And wishes to turn you into one?'

'Impossible!' Jaime said and chuckled.

She faced him. 'As my mother so often had reason to say, a man has limited eyesight; he can see a hundred faults in another, but not one in himself.'

'Your mother...'

'Yes?'

'Was very uncomplimentary about men.'

'She was married.' She spoke to Alvarez. 'What are you going to do about it?'

'What can I do?'

'If you have to ask, then there is nothing.'

'He's my senior.'

'You said he was an inspector, the same as you.'

'But Salas has put him in charge.'

'Does that entitle him to tell you to starve?'

'If I eat here every lunchtime, he'll moan like hell to Salas. He's that kind of man.'

'Invite him here to lunch.'

'Do what?'

'A man has only two interests in life and the less obnoxious one is his stomach. After this miserable inspector has eaten a meal I have cooked, he will no longer regard a sandwich as anything but a *rollo*.'

Alvarez and Jaime were astounded by her use of such an expression.

'If I'd said that...' Jaime began.

'It would have been as meaningless as most things you say. And you will not pour yourself another drink because I am about to serve lunch.'

'Enrique's just had another.'

'When a man has been as insulted as he has, he needs support.'

* * *

'You have enjoyed a very extended luncheon,' was Pocavi's greeting on his return.

Alvarez sat, his mind still like cotton wool because his siesta had been so short.

'I have been working on the papers from the safe. I am of the opinion there is proof of a direct connexion between the money paid regularly out of Vickers's account and the money received by Upton. Blackmail is the most obvious conclusion, but as you should have learned, first conclusions often fail the test of time. Am I correct that you have found nothing apart from the bank accounts to substantiate blackmail of Vickers?'

'Yes.'

'So there is a conundrum.'

He wasn't going to allow Pocavi to believe he had not foreseen what that was. 'Exactly. If—'

'Leaving aside the question of whether the beneficiary of blackmail would murder the person he was blackmailing, are you aware that uncovering motive often unlocks the facts of a case?'

'Of course.'

'Throughout my long and, I hesitate to add, successful career I have never been involved in a motiveless murder although, of course, I am fully aware that these do occur – a drunken brawl, mistaken identity, mental instability. If this was not an accident – and I agree with the superior chief, that is a big if – then neither was it manslaughter since an elaborate attempt was made to make it *appear* an accident. So motive becomes the most important feature of this investigation at the moment.'

'Which is why—'

'Kindly let me finish. You learned early in your investigation that Vickers frequently entertained married women in circumstances which might lead one to suspect each of having an affair with him.'

'The superior chief was reluctant to accept that.'

'Superior Chief Salas possesses a refined moral sense and therefore naturally is reluctant to accept the actions of those without any. You questioned the staff at Ca Na Pantella and learned that certain cars, each driven by a woman on her own, were frequently seen there. You identified the cars and questioned the wives concerned, and their husbands, and came to the conclusion that none of the husbands was a suspect. Do you believe you identified every car that has relevance to the case?'

'Yes.'

'Why?'

'The staff gave me the information.'

'You have not considered the possibility there were other cars about which you have not been told?'

'It's unlikely that between them the staff missed anyone. They always know what's going on.'

'They can be bribed to forget. You understand the point I am making?'

'No.'

'It was not a foolproof way of identifying all the married women Vickers entertained.'

'I should have used some lateral thinking?'

'I am sorry that the advantage of that so clearly escapes you. A further effort must be made to identify any husband who had reason to kill Vickers.'

'You are accepting he was murdered?'

'At the moment, the only way in which to establish the manner of death is negative. You follow what I am saying?'

'So long as you don't use words of more than one syllable.'

'It is always a pleasure to meet someone with a good sense of humour. Were there no errant wives whose visits to Ca Na Pantella were not described by the staff? Did none of the cuckolded husbands consider the betrayal to be of overwhelming consequence; did none of them lie when persuading you of his innocence? Can one be certain there was no other motive for Vickers's death?'

'I have uncovered no other.'

'And you will not, if death was accidental.'

Alvarez brought a pack of cigarettes out of his pocket.

'I should prefer you not to smoke in here. Passive smoking has been proven to be highly dangerous... I have decided to reorganize the investigation in order to bring it to a rapid conclusion. You have other cases in hand?'

'Of course, but only minor ones.'

'Nevertheless, they must be dealt with, so

you will investigate them. And you will speak to those who knew Vickers and encourage them to tell you all they can about him.'

'You're telling me you're completely taking over the investigation into Señor Vickers's death?'

'I'm sorry to have to do this, but as the superior chief said to me, for the sake of the island's reputation of peace, the case must be quickly cleared up and not left to drag on for months.'

'Which it would be if left to me?'

'I did not say that.'

'You inferred it.'

'An inference is drawn by the listener.'

'I am going to complain to the superior chief.'

'You will gain nothing by doing so.'

Alvarez brought a cigarette out of the pack still in his left hand and lit this before he left the room.

He went downstairs and along to the general room, which fortunately was empty. He dialled Palma, told the plum-voiced secretary he wished to speak to the superior chief.

'What is it?' Salas demanded.

'Señor, I have just been informed—'

'To whom am I speaking?'

'Inspector Alvarez.'

'Am I supposed to recognize the identity of every voice I hear?'

'But when I do say who I am, you tell me not to waste your time since your secretary has said who's calling.'

'You have an insolent habit of arguing unnecessarily. Just explain why you're phoning.'

'I have been informed by Inspector Pocavi that he is taking complete charge of the Vickers investigation and I am to be taken off it.'

'I am surprised it has taken him this long to find that necessary.'

'His rank is no higher than mine. I have done all the work...'

'Were you to be left in charge of the case, it would never be established whether death was due to murder or accident. Inspector Pocavi is intelligent, efficient, and motivated, so if the case is in his hands, it will very soon be solved.'

The line went dead.

He'd been relegated to listening to tittle-tattle because he was unintelligent, inefficient, and torpid.

'I've seen people look more cheerful at their own funeral,' the bartender said.

'They've reason to be cheerful; their troubles are behind them.'

'What's the tragedy? You forgot to buy a lottery ticket and your numbers came up?'

'I've been kicked where it hurts by a smooth, sarcastic, scheming shit.'

'You didn't kick him back?'

'He's the superior chief's favourite. Kick him and I'm history in the Cuerpo.'

'So what are you going to do?'

'What I'm bloody well told, I suppose.'

'That'll make a change.'

'You're a great comforter.'

'It's what I put in the glass that comforts and yours is empty.'

'I don't think I want another.'

'You're becoming psychotic,' the bartender said as he reached for the glass.

Eighteen

Dolores cleared the table of plates and cutlery, carried the tray through to the kitchen. Almost immediately, she returned to stand near Alvarez's chair. Jaime, who had expected his wife to remain in the kitchen, tried to make out he had not been about to pour himself another brandy.

'Are you ill, Enrique?' she asked.

He shook his head.

'Then there is more trouble?'

'A whole mountain of it. And that will become even greater because I returned home for lunch.'

'What has happened now?'

'I've been demoted.'

'How can that be,' Jaime asked, 'when there aren't any lower ranks in the Cuerpo?'

'Or less thoughtful husbands on the island,' she snapped. 'You have nothing to do but sit there? Then you can mend the fan in the kitchen.'

'I'm meeting Marcial in ten minutes.'

'In which bar?'

'In the Cloisters to discuss something important. Why are you women so suspicious and disbelieving? Marcial says his Teresa is just the same. Disbelieving everything he says.'

'And, no doubt, with equally good reason. How many times have you promised to mend the fan? Can one count the stars in the sky? Aiyee! My mother was so right when she said man was descended not from apes, but sloths.'

Jaime muttered something he was careful could not be understood, then left.

Dolores sat. 'What is the new trouble which has made you even more depressed?'

He told her.

'The superior chief will not listen to you? He does not understand how you must feel when he acts as he has?'

'He's not concerned with how I feel. He

judges me to be too incompetent to continue handling the case so Pocavi takes
over.'

'You are not incompetent.'

'I've got nowhere with the case.'

'You have tried as hard as you could.'

'And failed.'

'Are the little men from Madrid always
successful?'

'Probably. They are clever enough to have
been to universities. I am just a peasant.'

'And when there is a need to eat, who is
the more important? The clever man with
his degree or the peasant who grows the
food?'

'Until there is no food available, the question has little relevance.'

'Enrique, you sound as if you believe you
are beaten.'

'I am.'

'Never say such a thing.'

'Be a man, not a mouse?'

'Fight.'

'Authority never presents a stationary
target.' He stood. 'I must return to work.'

'In the state you are in, you need a good

siesta.'

'True, but that little bastard is just waiting to catch me doing something that will allow him to make a report to Salas that highlights how smart he is and how incompetent and lazy I am. And yet ... I suppose...'

'What?'

'Since he has stripped me of all responsibility except to clear up any local cases, which usually clear themselves, and collect tittle-tattle, my only immediate duty is to speak to all those who knew Señor Vickers; this will take much time and effort. If he should ring here...'

'I will tell him I have not seen you since you left at your usual time.'

'Don't let the kids know you're ready to lie on my behalf!'

'If I leave now to spend the afternoon with Margarita and do not return until after your siesta is over and you do leave, I shall be speaking the truth. That is always better.'

He crossed to the staircase and went up to his bedroom.

Since it was good tactics to be able to prove

at least part of what one claimed, Alvarez drove down to the port, parked, and walked the short distance to Carrer de Cardenal Rossell.

'How nice to see you again,' Mrs Sewell said. 'Come in and have a coffee.'

He sat in the sitting room. Through the opened window came the noise of traffic. Before the tourists had arrived in numbers, there would have been the sound of few cars, but the creakings and squeals of many mule carts. Now cars had become so numerous that streets had been made one-way and one seldom, if ever, saw a donkey cart. Had any previous generation seen such changes as his had?

'You're very serious,' she said as she returned with a tray bearing cups, saucers, milk, sugar, and spoons. 'Do help yourself.'

'I was thinking how times have altered, Señora.' He added milk and sugar to one of the cups of coffee.

'Haven't I told you to call me Lavinia?'

'I'm sorry.'

She put the tray down, lifted cup and saucer off it, sat. 'Times always have and

always will change and people will always
resent the changes. What do you consider to
be the greatest one you have experienced?'

'When I was young, the nearest doctor
was many kilometres away and one had to
pay to visit him, which many were unable to
do. Now there are medical centres so that
one goes there to see the doctor and does
not have to pay him. Who can tell how much
suffering that has prevented?'

'I'm so glad to hear you talk about something really important and not cars, television, travel. Now, tell me, is this a social
visit or an official one?'

'I need to talk to someone who knew
Señor Vickers; there is no one with whom I
would prefer to do so.'

'Flattery gains my full co-operation.'

'Sincerity, Señora, not flattery.'

'But what more can I tell you about Jasper
than I have previously?'

'Probably nothing.'

'You come here with questions and say
you don't expect to learn anything from my
answers. Surely you didn't need an excuse
to come and see me?'

'I needed to come and see you in order to have an excuse.'

'If you're trying to mystify me, you're succeeding.'

'An excuse to allow me to have enjoyed a siesta.'

'You must be the only Mallorquin who needs an excuse to do that. Once again, you're not telling me the truth – or at least, not the full truth.'

'This time I can assure you it's the whole truth.'

'Then I have to believe you... But there's something I want to say.'

He waited.

'It will probably make you consider me an interfering, silly old woman.'

'Nothing could do that.'

'It's about Joan. People are talking more and more... People who don't understand because they haven't the qualities to be able to do so. They believe the obvious and seldom have the wit to wonder if the obvious could be wrong. You know Joan Langley.'

'Yes.'

'You also know she visited Jasper so often

that people assumed the obvious?'

'Yes.'

'They never stopped to think what kind of person she is and so never realized that for her, loyalty is next to godliness. She loves her husband and would never betray him with another man. But the rumour that she had a prolonged affair with Jasper has taken an even stronger hold and now people are suggesting Gavin killed Jasper. It's appalling nonsense. She did see Jasper quite often, because sailing is a passion for her and he welcomed her skills – and needed them if he was not to appear a fool. She would not have let him touch her.'

'Señora – Lavinia, after I had spoken to Señor and Señora Langley, I understood that she had never allowed Vickers the slightest favour and therefore her husband had had no cause to kill Vickers.'

'Thank God. I had to speak because the thought you might believe she was Jasper's lover made me feel sick. I should have understood you are far too knowledgeable about people to make such a terrible mistake.'

★ ★ ★

Later that evening, Jaime and Dolores had gone up to bed – after she had warned Alvarez not to drink too much – and he was alone, facing the television and looking at a film but not really taking it in. When a man was left without pride, too much alcohol was never enough. He refilled his glass.

Pocavi had no right to scorn him and feed that scorn to Salas. In truth, his work had not been all failure. Wasn't it he who had appreciated the significance of the phone calls to Mahon as well as the manner of the two deaths? That Vickers had visited Upton in Menorca? But it was true that all his work had failed to lead to success. And yet was every criminal case solved? Of course not. Was Pocavi as smart as he believed himself to be? Of course not.

His glass was again empty. He studied the bottle of Soberano. But a wise man knew when to call a halt. So just a very small one. Fifteen minutes later, he decided to go to bed and stood, hastily catching hold of the edge of the table for support.

He climbed the stairs slowly and carefully,

chuckled when he thought how confused everyone would be if he fell and cracked his head on something solid. Would they consider the possibility that he had been murdered because he was almost up with the murderer? Would they tie themselves into knots trying to deduce the truth? He entered his bedroom, undressed without too much difficulty, climbed into bed, switched off the overhead light.

Sleep was a blessing meant to allow one to escape the bitter world of reality. Unfortunately, he suffered a nightmare in which he appeared before the Inquisition, the two judges of which were Salas and Pocavi. He awoke just before the wood piled around his lower body was lit.

He went along to the bathroom, returned to bed, switched off the light again. To his resentful annoyance, his mind would not recompose itself for sleep, but insisted on referring to his part in the investigation into the deaths of Vickers and Upton. Could he have been more alert? Were there leads to be followed which he had not been sharp enough to identify? Had he been naive when he had accepted that Joan Langley had been telling the truth, that Lavinia Sewell's confirmation of this was to be accepted without question? Women were ever deceivers. Perhaps... If... Possibly... Suppose...

Lavinia had said something that had seemed to be of some significance, but when he tried to recall what it had been, he found it difficult to remember anything much about his visit to her.

'I expected you to return yesterday evening to report to me,' Pocavi said next morning as Alvarez entered the post.

'It was getting so late by the time I finished work.'

'Too late by whose standards? Where were you all afternoon and evening?'

Alvarez crossed to the second desk and sat.

'I am unsurprised you find difficulty in answering.'

'I spent some of the time in the port, enjoying the beauty of the bay as I tried to make sense of everything known in the two cases. I have always found that when one meets a mental brick wall, the only thing to do is to relax and let the mind wander among the improbabilities and the impossibilities.'

'I have difficulty in accepting what you're telling me.'

'You are calling me a liar?'

'You will put your own interpretation on my words.'

'Ring my home, speak to my cousin, ask her if she saw me during the afternoon or evening.'

'I do not wish to suggest to a third party that I cannot trust my colleague.' Pocavi picked up a pencil and fiddled with it. 'Before I left Palma, the superior chief spoke at some length about you. I believed that, for once, he had to be mistaken since it seemed he must be exaggerating. Since then I have learned that it was I who was mistaken in disbelieving him.' He put the pencil down. 'Did you manage to find time, in between your communing with nature, to question anyone?'

'Yes.'

'Did you learn anything fresh?'

'No.'

'Very well. You can now return to your local cases.'

As Alvarez left the building, he considered whether Pocavi would pause from his work to enter a café and decided he definitely would not. He walked to the old square, passed the many tourists who were able to enjoy the pleasure of doing nothing but drink, and started to walk down the steps to the road and Club Llueso. Two young shapely women wearing bikinis passed him as they climbed up.

The bartender nodded a hullo and, without being asked, filled a container with ground coffee, fixed this in the espresso machine, poured a generous brandy, and put the glass down on the counter.

'Do you know what I've just seen?' Alvarez asked.

'A pink elephant.'

'Two young women in the square, wearing just bikinis.'

'I've seen 'em in floppy blouses and real short shorts, but not bikinis,' said the bartender regretfully.

'Gets a man thinking.'

'Only if he's young enough.'

'One's never too old.'

'If you can think the likes of them would look twice at you, you're living in a dream.' The bartender moved away to pour out the coffee, which he then placed in front of Alvarez.

'You can be a miserable sod!'

'That's what keeps me smiling.'

Alvarez carried glass, cup and saucer over to a window seat. As he drank, he looked out at the moving crowd. Everyone was now casually but soberly dressed. He finished the brandy, walked to the bar for a refill, returned to his seat. Before the tourists, only a *puta* would have worn clothing that might reveal any part of herself that would intrigue a man. Now, women walked about in almost nothing. In years to come, perhaps they would dispense with any clothes at all on a warm sunny day. Or maybe changing fashion and morals would demand women once more be fully clothed in public so that, ironically, greater excitement might be gained from far less.

He poured what remained of the brandy into the coffee and now remembered part of his previous day's conversation with Lavinia Sewell. A bikini-clad blonde in the centre of the village represented as great a change as health centres – though the benefits of the one were doubtful. What would her opinion be? Probably sharp and to the point. He remembered trying to recall something she had said when his mind had not been at its clearest. But what that had been continued to evade him. So he forgot the question. And, in the strange way in which the human mind worked, he suddenly remembered the answer. She had remarked that people never doubted the obvious, and that, whatever the apparent circumstances, Joan Langley would never have committed adultery...

She had spoken truly; people did accept the obvious without question. Perhaps even he, trained by time to disbelieve, had been guilty of doing so... He silently swore with Mallorquin velocity. It had seemed so obvious that the sheet of newspaper found in Vickers's safe had been kept because of the photograph of the topless woman. As

Alvarez he had judged her assets, he had not asked himself why a man who enjoyed the favours of many mistresses, when pornography was on open sale, would have hidden it in the safe. When the question was asked, the answer was obvious. It was the article below the photograph that had been so important.

Nineteen

It was 9.15 in the morning when Pocavi hurried into the office and stood in front of Alvarez's desk. 'Are you incapable of observing rules?' he demanded.

Alvarez looked up. Gone were the sweet tones and gentle words hiding the greasy, fawning sycophant; now he faced a man who was bitterly annoyed and no longer even trying to be pleasant.

'Well?'

'I'm not certain what you're talking about.'

'You know very well.'

'Then I know, but I do not know that I do.'

'You think acting smart will do you any good?'

'That's usually considered more advantageous than acting stupid.'

'Did I tell you I was taking charge of the investigation into the deaths of Vickers and Upton?'

'The first, yes, but I rather thought the Menorquin Cuerpo would continue to investigate the latter. Unless, of course, they seek your experience.'

'Don't try and take the piss out of me.'

'That is something I certainly would rather not do.'

'You're not fit to be a typist in the Cuerpo.'

'That seems reasonable since I cannot type with more than two fingers.'

'What is the most important rule any junior officer has to follow?'

'To eat sandwiches at lunchtime?'

'To keep his senior informed of everything he has done and intends to do. Have you asked me for permission to contact the English police?'

'I can't remember doing so.'

'Don't try and tell me you'd forgotten an officer is not permitted to be in touch with the police of another country without his senior's permission.'

'Then I won't.'

'You admit you did not ask me for permission to do so?'

'You are not my senior officer.'

'Then you made the request directly to the superior chief, without any reference to me?'

'In fact, no, I didn't.'

'I imagine he'll be grateful for that. It should provide him with a valid reason for doing what he has wished to do for a long time. To have you retired, should there not be sufficient valid evidence to have you sacked.'

'I'd prefer the first because then I will have my pension and I can grow tomatoes with a flavour.'

'You are going to learn this isn't a matter for jest. The superior chief has told me to bring you to his office tomorrow morning.'

'In handcuffs?'

'He asked me if I could begin to understand how you came to be accepted into the Cuerpo. I told him it was as much a mystery to me as to him.'

★ ★ ★

Salas's office reflected rank. It was large, airy and almost luxuriously furnished; notable features were the framed photograph of him being honoured by the king and the estate desk at which he sat, a Spanish antique made of mahogany and beautifully inlaid.

He was a short man who resented the height of others; he was beginning to bald and combed his black hair in a way he hoped would hide that fact; he had brown eyes, a long nose, and a pencil moustache above a narrow-lipped mouth; he suffered from a form of rhinitis which caused him constantly to touch his nose with a handkerchief, making it seem an affectation; he was known as being extraordinarily prudish – in fact, it was not disgust which caused him to dislike any mention of a sexual nature, but resentment; his wife had denied him marital rights after the birth of their second child and, as he learned, his authority did not extend into the bedroom.

He greeted Pocavi warmly, nodded curtly at Alvarez. 'You may sit.'

They sat.

'Before I deal with the very serious matter which has brought you here, I will deal with another which, in its own way, also is important. Where is your report?'

'Report, Señor?'

'Clearly, of such small importance as far as you are concerned, you have forgotten all about it. I am referring to the monthly report on events in your area which you claim to have sent by post, yet which never arrived, and which you then said you would forward by fax, but which equally has failed to reach me.'

'As I'm sure I mentioned, the fax has been giving me trouble...'

'Because it disallows the excuse of an incompetent postal service? I will deal with the matter later. Now, we will move on.

'Inspector Pocavi tried very hard to enjoy a normal working relationship with you, but regretfully reported he was forced to decide this was impossible and you were more of a hindrance than an asset to his investigation. As a consequence, he told you to resume normal duties only. Yet it seems that, contrary to his orders, you have continued to

concern yourself with the investigation into
the death of Señor Vickers.'

'I did pursue one lead, Señor.'

'Have you studied the rules governing the
work and behaviour of members of the
Cuerpo?'

'Of course.'

'Then why does your every action seem to
make it clear you have no idea what those
rules are?'

'That's not fair.'

'Life is not fair or I should not have had to
suffer you under my command. Were you
aware that an officer must not apply for help
from the force of another country without a
senior's permission to do so?'

'Yes, but—'

'There are no buts. You were either aware
of the rule or you were not. Since you admit
you were, how do you explain the fact you
contacted the English police without a word
to me or to Inspector Pocavi?'

'Inspector Pocavi is not my senior.'

'I informed you he would be in charge and
therefore it was obvious any such request
had to be made to him. Why did you ignore

procedure?'

'Because I was afraid he would not understand the reason for my request and therefore would refuse to pass it on to you.'

'Señor...' Pocavi began angrily.

'You do not need to object to what he has
just said. The stupidity of his words is
obvious. Alvarez, you have constantly given
me reason to doubt your ability to do anything correctly. This latest breach of procedure by you, the last in a long line, means
I am forced to present to the Director General a report on your behaviour and ability,
together with Inspector Pocavi's critical
assessment of same. In summation, I will
have to add that both I and Inspector Pocavi
respectfully suggest your absence from the
Cuerpo is advisable. Have you anything to
say?'

'Yes, Señor.'

'Well?'

'I would suggest that before you do that,
you first learn what was the nature of my
request to the English police.'

Salas, remembering the past, was suddenly uneasy.

Pocavi said, 'Whatever the nature – and my short experience of your work suggests it can be of no account – you should not have made that request without reference to me.'

'And have you ignore it because it required imagination to appreciate?' Alvarez replied.

'I am interested to learn that you consider imagination more important than facts, since there is finally the explanation of something which I could not understand – your extraordinary degree of incompetence. You have still not learned that a case is solved by facts, not imagination.'

'Sometimes it is.'

Pocavi turned to Salas. 'Señor, I feel this is getting us nowhere. Inspector Alvarez is clearly unable to appreciate the qualities his job demands and is trying to evade the consequences of his insolent breach of rules.'

'I think,' Salas said carefully, 'we should let the inspector continue. What is the absurdity, Alvarez?'

'That a man like Vickers would keep the page of a newspaper in a safe simply because it had the photograph of a topless young lady.'

'At a time like this, you revert to your perverted fantasies?'

'One sees naked breasts everywhere – in magazines, on the beaches, on the television. They have long since ceased to offer the attraction of the forbidden. Of course, the photograph was not the reason for the retention of the newspaper in the safe. It was the article below the photograph that was of interest.

'With journalistic enthusiasm, this claimed that new forensic techniques would solve many old crimes which had so far remained unsolved.'

'Why should anyone find that significant?' Pocavi demanded angrily.

'By identifying how irrational it was to accept that Vickers would have been keeping a page from a newspaper in a safe solely because it contained a photograph of a topless woman.'

'I was in charge of the investigation. You should have pointed that out.'

'I would have done, but you scorned all my efforts and then took me off the case.'

'You deliberately—'

Salas interrupted him. 'That's enough. Alvarez, you will continue.'

'It took me rather a long time to appreciate the significance of that absurdity, but then I had been making the common mistake of accepting the obvious. I think Inspector Pocavi must agree that this is all too easily done. Anyway, if Señor Vickers's death was murder, as I was certain, it was necessary to identify motive and the bitter hatred of a cuckolded husband provided a very strong, but fallacious one. Then, after the death of Señor Upton there was a second possible motive: blackmail. As you know, Señor, I worked all hours of the day and night – which is why the report has not reached you since I could not get the fax to work properly...'

'Forget the damned report and continue.'

'Yes, Señor. I decided to try to uncover further possible motives. That is when I realized I had been misleading myself by accepting the obvious. Unfortunately, Inspector Pocavi did not reach the same conclusion – it is, of course, not easy to accept that one has been blind.

'I had passport photos of both Vickers and Upton and sent these to England with the request to check whether they might have any connexion with major unsolved crimes. I had considered the rule requiring me to gain permission to do what I intended, but regretfully felt certain Inspector Pocavi would not understand my reason for doing this.

'England replied quickly. There was evidence to believe both men, under their real names, had been involved in a violent crime which had taken place some time before. Vickers – to maintain the names by which we knew them – had been the managing director of a company that specialized in security. They owned secure storage space in three of the major airports in the United Kingdom and had secured contracts with foreign companies in France, Italy, Spain, and Turkey, to accept and hold sterling which had been changed for euros and liras by tourists in those countries. Until collected, this sterling was protected by the most sophisticated security devices and by guards.

'Vickers was a dedicated womanizer and had run into very large debt pursuing his pleasures. Seduction is difficult when a man cannot overcome a woman's reluctance with the luxuries that persuade—'

'There is no need to pursue the matter.'

'No, Señor. So he had to find another source of income. As managing director of the company, he had full knowledge of the security systems. But he was no master criminal and so the plan remained only in his mind, until he met Upton.

'Upton had a criminal record and for him, violence was a tool to be used when needed. How, where, and when he met Vickers is not known, but some time after doing so, a large consignment of higher denomination notes was due to arrive at Heathrow on a Monday, sufficiently late that it could not be cleared before the morning. That night, Upton, with one companion, drove up to the store in a stolen company's van and, with the aid of the information Vickers had provided, gained entrance without any trouble. The guards, covered by guns, were bound and gagged. Just before the loading was completed, one of the guards managed partially to free his hands and was trying to reach one of the many alarm activators when Upton shot him.

'The total amount stolen was large and ensured the case became headline news. It took the police little time to decide there had been an inside informer, even less to name Vickers. But before they could gather sufficient evidence, he disappeared. They did their best to trace him, but leads failed to lead, informants failed to inform, and Interpol proved unable to help.

'Following my request to the British police, and the information I provided, they have asked us to provide any further evidence we have that might be of use to them. They also kindly thanked us for helping them and congratulated you, Señor, on having so efficient a team – naturally, I had explained that you were in charge of the investigation. They also said they would be following up their thanks to us with a congratulatory letter to the director general.'

'Oh!'

'I imagine he will be very pleased by that.'

Salas made a strange sound that denoted agreement, or something.

'I would suggest that we can now try to make sense of what happened here and on Menorca – I imagine that Superior Chief Calafat will also be grateful for the help you will be able to give them in closing their case. To work out what did happen will unfortunately need the use of some imagination, since we can never know all the facts for certain. I say unfortunately because I know Inspector Pocavi dislikes the use of imagination and has pursued his very successful career without it, but in my far less successful one I have occasionally found the judicious use of imagination to be of great advantage. And I would respectfully point out that in this case, but for my use of imagination, we would not now be able to speak of success. And perhaps my experience of dealing with foreigners and their strange ways has played a small part in my – I mean our success.

'Vickers was a clever man, but very nervous. From the beginning, he had accepted that if there were a robbery, suspicion must fall on him and his life would be so closely investigated he would be unlikely to escape justice. So he reasoned that only by leaving the country and living under a carefully constructed false name abroad would he remain free. He also identified that the reason for the police's success in arresting many guilty men was that they betrayed their guilt by publishing their success too openly. So the man Upton brought into the robbery would never know Vickers had any part in it and Upton would not have immediate access to his share of the robbery's proceeds. These would be lodged in a bank well away from the petty restrictions of the Inland Revenue and a regular payment would be made to Upton, who had agreed to live in Menorca where he would be well away from the English police and close enough to Mallorca for Vickers to keep track of him. The money he was paid by Vickers would allow him to lead a carefree life, but not in such luxury to make people wonder how a man of his background could afford to spend so lavishly. And, of course, from

Upton's point of view, Vickers was bound to continue the payments for fear that if he didn't, he would be betrayed.

'Vickers read in that newspaper page I found in the safe that the English police were, thanks to new techniques, confident of solving many hitherto unsolved crimes. He feared this would result in he and Upton being uncovered and forced to return to England to stand trial. Because the robbery had been planned by him, even though Upton had shot the guard and Vickers was not present, he would be charged as an accessory to murder. Ever more nervous, he made contact with Upton and increasingly sought assurance that his fears were unjustified; to a man in fear, reassurance can be more important than the validity of the reassurance.

'Unsettled and alarmed by the consequences of Vickers's fears, Upton became afraid that Vickers would become so frightened, so certain he would be arrested, that he would try to lessen his punishment by confessing his part of the robbery, while insisting he had not known Upton was armed or that he intended to use the gun if necessary.

'Upton decided his future safety lay in the death of Vickers. More brawn than brain, however he decided to make the murder look like suicide. He would arrive at Ca Na Pantella when the staff were unlikely to be there, would claim something potentially dangerous had occurred which would ensure Vickers, panicking, would let him into the house. Once inside, he put a knife to Vickers's throat, bound his hands together, forced him up to the sitting room. By now, frighteningly certain of Upton's intention, Vickers fought wildly. Enraged by the opposition, Upton, who suffered a short fuse and seldom thought ahead when angry, forced the neck of the first bottle into his mouth, careless of the damage caused, then did the same with the second bottle. Certain it would look like Vickers had been drunk and apparently so befuddled he fell, eager to vent his anger at the resistance, Upton pushed him over the balustrade. He removed the masking tape. He searched the house to get his hands on all the money he could, either directly or indirectly by forgery after identifying bank accounts and other capital, found that everything must be in the safe which he lacked the skill to force. If his plan had not called for Vickers to die by accidental death for his own safety, no doubt he would have trashed the house in his even greater anger at his own stupidity for not having learned the combination to the safe before he killed Vickers, even if that would have provided obvious signs of torture. Vickers had shown him that a man with money could disappear. He left the house having taken the key from the front door and locking that from the outside.

'On his arrival in Menorca, his mind must have been a maelstrom. He no longer had to fear being betrayed, but by his own actions he had made certain he had lost all the monetary benefits of their crime. At such a time, it was his nature to drink heavily in an attempt to find temporary consolation. Ironically, he drank so excessively that he lost his balance on the dangerous stone staircase, fell and suffered fatal injuries...'

'This is taking imagination to absurd

lengths,' Pocavi said.

'Inspector Alvarez,' Salas said curtly, 'has an imaginative approach to his work, which is often successful and is something you might be well advised to develop yourself, Inspector Pocavi.'

When he returned from his victorious meeting with Salas and Pocavi, Alvarez had to park further from home than he would have liked since that was at least a couple of hundred metres away, and in such heat, to walk any distance was potentially danger-ous. Nevertheless he was smiling as he pick-ed up the two bottles from the passenger seat and strode along the road. There were times when the world was golden. Pocavi had looked as if he had swallowed some-thing poisonous.

Jaime sat at the table in the dining/sitting room, wondering whether Dolores would claim it was too early for a pre-meal drink. Alvarez put the two bottles down on the table. 'Hors d'Age to whet our appetites, and Domecq Domain to honour the feast we are about to eat.'

Jaime looked at the bottles, then at Alvarez. 'Have you been robbing a bank?'

'Something much more enjoyable than that.'

Dolores came through the bead curtain. 'And what has proved so enjoyable?' she asked in imperious tones.

'Earlier, I met—'

'Sadly, there is no need to explain further. A mule does not grow smaller ears. You met a young foreign woman who has sufficient sense of humour to lead you to believe she welcomed the advances of a man clearly old enough to be her grandfather. Aiyee! The good Lord was not thinking when He created man.' She swept back into the kitchen.

'But the Devil was, when he created woman,' Alvarez said quietly as he reached for the *coñac*.